"Well, as I see it, my oven is your problem."

It was becoming a struggle to remain civil about being roused out of bed by a flame-haired, loud-mouthed tornado in the middle of the night. "Not according to my paperwork. And believe me, Miss Hopkins, I read my paperwork."

"Well, if I can't open my bakery, I can't earn money. And if I can't earn money, then I can't pay my rent. So, unless you want to start off the year badly, I reckon it is your problem."

The Southern phraseology in her East Coast accent was just absurd. He glared at her. "Exactly *what part* of New Jersey are you from?"

That stopped her. "Exactly how much do you know about me?"

Exactly too much. And none of it prepared him for this. "I'm going back to bed now."

"By all means. I won't need any supervision from you. I'll just slip in and slip out, moving batches in and out of your oven. You'll never even know I'm there."

Oh, he doubted that.

Books by Allie Pleiter

Love Inspired

My So-Called Love Life
The Perfect Blend
*Bluegrass Hero
*Bluegrass Courtship
*Bluegrass Blessings

*Kentucky Corners

Steeple Hill Books

Bad Heiress Day
Queen Esther & the
  Second Graders of Doom

Love Inspired Historical

Masked by Moonlight

ALLIE PLEITER

Enthusiastic but slightly untidy mother of two, RITA® Award finalist Allie Pleiter writes both fiction and nonfiction. An avid knitter and unreformed chocoholic, she spends her days writing books, drinking coffee and finding new ways to avoid housework. Allie grew up in Connecticut, holds a BS in Speech from Northwestern University, spent fifteen years in the field of professional fundraising. She lives with her husband, children and a Havanese dog named Bella in the suburbs of Chicago, Illinois.

Bluegrass Blessings
Allie Pleiter

Steeple
Hill®

Published by Steeple Hill Books™

STEEPLE HILL BOOKS

Steeple Hill®

Recycling programs for this product may not exist in your area.

ISBN-13: 978-0-373-87538-2

BLUEGRASS BLESSINGS

www.SteepleHill.com

Printed in U.S.A.

See, the former things have taken place,
and new things I declare; before they
spring into being I announce them to you.
—*Isaiah* 42:9

For Jeff
And he knows why

Acknowledgments

Every author needs the right ingredients to cook
up the perfect novel. Attorney Donna Craft Cain
helped me get the legal details in order, while
Dr. Caroline Wolfe made sure the medical facts
were in correct. If I could send Cookiegrams of
my own, they'd go out to my husband, children,
editor Krista Stroever and agent Karen Solem for
their ongoing support. I'm well aware that living
with an author—professionally or personally—is
no piece of cake. Especially this author. And lastly,
I'd be nowhere without the astounding guidance
of my Lord and the amazing support of the readers
who've made Middleburg one of their favorite
places to visit. You're great blessings, one and all.

Chapter One

"You can't do this." Dinah Hopkins glared mercilessly at the oven knobs. "I own you. You work for me and insubordination of any kind will not be permitted. *Capiche?*"

Her New York mobster impersonation failed to impress, for the pilot light still stared at her with one blue, unblinking eye. For lack of a better solution, she whacked the side of the cold oven with her rolling pin. *Whacked.* That was a gangster term, right?

"Whacked, as in end of life. As in light this minute or it's the end of my life, buster." Dinah fiddled with another knob or two, which had worked last week to get the fickle thing started, and checked the gas connection. "All's well, you iron beast, you've got gas and flame but what I need is heat. So *heat.* I can't exactly run a bakery with a microwave. Bakeries have ovens. Nice, obedient, toasty ovens."

The blue unblinking eye mocked her. Okay, let's try a little tenderness. "C'mon, baby, you know you want to. It's a brand new year. You see that dough over there just begging to be sticky buns? You can do that. You're the one who makes it happen. Let's get cooking." Dinah stroked the side of one burner as if she really could tickle an oven under the chin. She straightened up, blew a lock of her bright red hair out of her eyes, and listened to the hideous silence. No ticking sound, no heating metal, no hot oven.

No response. "I'm your master and I said 'heat!'"

"Don't you mean mistress?"

Dinah jumped at the unexpected male voice, spinning around ready to wield her rolling pin upon the intruder. The thing was large enough to be a weapon, that's for sure. She dropped it on her toe once and limped for a week. She pointed it now at the dark stranger standing in her doorway. For a misguided robber dumb enough to enter a business with the lights on at two in the morning, he sure looked calm. And he was barefoot. And what was with the T-shirt and sweatpants? Didn't criminals wear black cat-suits? "Who are you and how did you get in here?"

The man yawned. "Could you put that thing down?" He reached into one pocket.

"Not a chance, buster." Dinah waved the rolling pin around to let him know just how serious she was about breaking a rib or two with it. She lunged for his hand just as he…pulled his glasses out of his pocket and held them out.

"Glasses," he said, fixing the expensive-looking tortoise shell frames onto his face. "Not firearms." Now he looked even less like a criminal. More like an accountant home sick with the flu.

"You've got ten seconds to tell me who you are." Dinah hoped that even in flip-flops, she could outrun him to the police station if he tried anything. Especially after she threw the rolling pin to bruise his trespassing little shins.

He scratched his stubbly chin. He had thick, dark hair. "Do you realize what time it is?"

"Time for you to get out of my bakery before I call the police. I'm sure *they* know what time it is."

"Sandy said you opened the bakery at six, maybe started baking at four. That was bad enough, but it's *two*. That's just not acceptable, no matter what you may have done in the past, so let's get that out on the table right now."

Sandy Burnside owned the building next door and hers as well. *Oh no.* Dinah put down the rolling pin and groaned. Sandy evidently did have a new tenant. A trespassing boor who decided it was okay to order perfect strangers around. "You're Sandy's new tenant? How'd you get in here?"

"Can I reach in my pocket again without the risk of pummeling?" The man did so and drew out a key. That still didn't explain anything. "I thought I heard something strange going on."

"My coming to work is strange?" Great. Not another one of those "the world is my territory and I must save the day" types. Dinah Hopkins was no damsel in distress and she surely didn't take to being treated like one in her own kitchen.

He yawned. "Someone assaulting an appliance in clown clothes at two in the morning is *not* strange?"

Dinah felt a surge of regret for the purple tank top and red striped pajama pants she currently wore. She always came down from her apartment upstairs—she had a direct stairway in the back—to start the ovens and put the first batch of buns in while she was still in her pajamas. "Some stranger sneaking into my bakery at two in the morning is strange enough. Once more, for the record, *who are you?*"

"Cameron Rollings. Your new neighbor. I moved in above Mr. MacCarthy's office next door."

"I can't say I care for your version of neighborliness,

Mr. Rollings. And do you want to tell me why Sandy chose to hand over my bakery keys to a total stranger?"

He raked his fingers through his unruly hair and straightened up. "Because I'm also your new landlord. I bought this building from Sandy last week while you were on vacation."

"You *what?*" He winced. She hadn't really thought she yelled that loud given her state of shock. When Sandy had casually mentioned wanting to sell off some of her real estate holdings some weeks back, Dinah had started saving. She couldn't put away much, but in another year, she might be able to make a small downpayment on the space that held her bakery and apartment. She'd never expected Sandy to sell so fast. While she was gone. To this guy. *I hate him already. Sorry, Lord, but he stole my bakery. That's not fair.*

"I bought this building. I'm staying in Sandy's other apartment, the one above MacCarthy's office, while I build a house on some of the other land I bought from her further out of town. So, I'm your neighbor for just a while but your landlord from here on in." He took a step toward her, adjusting his glasses. Even at this hour and in sweats, he had a well-mannered look about him—something in the precision of his haircut, the elegance of his glasses, the way he carried himself. He looked like the kind of guy who wore a tie to work every day and got his shirts done at the dry cleaner.

Lord, you know how those suit-and-tie types make me break out in hives. Why didn't I talk to Sandy about this before now? Now I'll never own the bakery outright. Not fair! Not fair! The plan was for me to buy the bakery and own my own building!

"I had planned to come down and introduce myself properly," he continued with a hint of a smile. "You know, in the daylight. Like normal people."

"Yeah, we all see how well that plan turned out, don't we? How come Sandy sold to an out-of-towner?"

"It was a sudden thing. Anyway, formal introductions and residency requirements aren't needed to buy property in New York. Is this a Kentucky thing I didn't know about?" He yawned again. "I don't suppose you've got any coffee on?"

Dinah glared at his dodging of the question. "I wasn't planning on company. The bakery coffee machines take half an hour to heat up. My little, fast coffeepot's upstairs. Where I *live*. Where I go back to get dressed for the day after the oven turns on. *When* the oven turns on, that is." She spun in a chaotic circle, grabbing a fistful of hair in one hand. "But it's no business of yours how I start my day. Come back at six when we open.... Hey, wait a minute, it *is* your business. Okay, Mr....what's your name again?"

"Rollings. Cameron Rollings."

Dinah straightened up. "Mr. Rollings, sir, my oven is broken. That's a landlord thing, isn't it? You own the place, you've gotta fix my oven, right?"

Rollings came over and sat on one of the stainless steel stools that stood next to the work counter. "Under normal circumstances, that'd be true. But your lease with Sandy states that you merely rent the space and all the specialized bakery appliances are your responsibility."

He was right. She'd completely forgotten about that because nothing had ever broken in the nearly year and a half she'd been running the Taste and See Bakery. That didn't really change matters, because as it stood, there wasn't anything she could do to get things baking in time to open today. *Why is it the world always goes to pieces my first day back from vacation?*

"On the other hand," he said, "if the oven in your apartment breaks, I guess that *is* my problem."

Her oven. She *did* have another oven! Sure, it was about one-third the size, but it was better than nothing. "My kitchen oven works. I could put some of this in there."

"So go put some of these…" He pointed to the tray of dough on the counter with one eyebrow raised.

"Sticky buns."

"Sticky buns in your apartment oven. I suppose I can see if there's anything to be done down here. For the sake of my future sleeping opportunities."

Dinah grabbed one of the two trays of dough, then stopped. "You can't."

He exhaled. "I know I'm not exactly the Maytag repairman…"

"You're barefoot. You can't. Regulations. You've got to have shoes on."

"Fine, I'll go upstairs and…"

Dinah reached down and pulled the fuchsia flip-flops off her feet and handed them to Rollings. "Here, wear these."

He stared at them. Sure, they had polka dots on the soles, but it wasn't like she was asking him to walk down the street in them. Slowly, as if they might inflict pain once applied, he took them from her. "And what are you going to wear?"

"I'm going upstairs to my apartment. I've got thirty-four more pairs up there, so chances are I'll find something."

Cameron found himself in an empty kitchen in the middle of the night, kneeling in front of an iron stove that looked as if it had lived through World War One, in pink flip-flops.

The new year was not off to a good start.

If anyone had told him even two months ago that he'd find himself in this circumstance, he might have called security and had them thrown out of his office.

Until, of course, his boss had called security and had Cameron thrown out of his own office. Funny thing, those bosses. They don't take kindly to being told their companies are corrupt. Not at Landemere Properties where Cameron worked—*ahem, used* to work—before he was told, in terms persuasive enough to make an employment attorney salivate, that his desk should be emptied and his resignation should be on the boss's desk within the hour.

You know, Lord, when I said that prayer asking what to do about the moral problems I was having with work? I wasn't really asking to leave my job. Or the state.

Cameron was just pondering his new sorry circumstances when Dinah Hopkins returned. In a lime green T-shirt slightly nicer than what she'd had on earlier, jeans and beaded green flip-flops. Maybe the woman really did own three dozen pairs—the greens matched exactly. She brushed her hands on the legs of her jeans. "Did you get it going?"

Other than stare at the iron monstrosity and twiddle a few knobs, Cameron realized he hadn't done anything. He was more of a microwave-frozen food kind of guy—he couldn't even remember the last time he'd turned on the oven in his old apartment. "Nothing doing. The pilot light's on, though."

"Well," she said sitting back on one hip with her arms

crossed, "I know *that*." She paused for a moment, running a finger absentmindedly through a lock of red hair. That couldn't be her real color, could it? Tomato-red like that? Then again, with those freckles, maybe it could. It wasn't like anything else about her was subtle. "Okay, then," she said abruptly, grabbing the remaining tray of sticky buns. "We'll have to use yours, too."

"What?"

"You. Your oven. Between the two ovens, I might be able to get enough buns and muffins baking to see me through the morning."

"Oh, no."

"Hey, you're up and all."

He reached under his glasses to rub his eyes. "I don't want to be." She parked her hands on her hips. He guessed she thought she was giving him a fierce look, but he'd seen far fiercer any given workday—her "ferocity" was mostly just entertaining. Like he'd just been launched into a bluegrass *I Love Lucy* episode without his consent. "This oven, as I just said, is not my problem to solve. I was merely trying to be helpful, but you look very resourceful—I'm sure you can get by on your own." He reached down to remove the hideous flip-flops, which didn't even make it halfway down his feet anyway, and handed them back. "I'm going back to bed, Miss Hopkins."

She put her hand out to stop the transfer of footwear. "You know my name?"

Cameron yawned again. "It did come up in the real estate transaction. Pertinent detail and all."

She pushed the flip-flops back toward him. "Well, as I see it, my oven is your problem."

It was becoming a struggle to remain civil about being roused out of bed by a flame-haired, loud-mouthed tornado in the middle of the night. "Not according to my paperwork. And believe me, Miss Hopkins, I read my paperwork." He thrust the pink monstrosities back in her direction.

"Well, if I can't open my bakery, I can't earn money. And if I can't earn money, then I can't pay my rent. So, unlessen you want to start off the year badly, I reckon it is your problem."

The Southern phraseology in her East Coast accent was just absurd. He glared at her. "Exactly *what part* of New Jersey are you from?"

That stopped her. "Exactly how much do you know about me?"

Exactly too much. And none of it prepared me for this. "I'm going back to bed now."

"By all means. I won't need any supervision from you. I'll just slip in and slip out, moving batches in and out of your oven. You'll never even know I'm there."

Oh, he doubted that. "No."

"Look, do you understand the concept of a bakery? It generally involves baked goods. That means baking. And you know, Mr. I'll-just-show-up-in-the-middle-of-the-night-and-scare-the-pants-off-my-new-tenant, my day is off to a really bad start."

Cameron took off his glasses and gave her his most domineering I-am-immovable-on-the-subject look. "And you know, I can't *imagine* what that feels like."

That set her back a bit. As if she'd just realized most of the civilized world didn't take kindly to rising so painfully early. So early it was actually still *late*. The pity was just a flash across her features, replaced almost immediately by a sharp scowl. "Well, fine, then. Be like that. Just what kind of heartless beast did Sandy sell to, anyway?"

"Her *nephew*," he shot back. He hadn't intended to let her know that just yet, but his growing exasperation pulled it out of him. Aunt Sandy told him Dinah could be a handful.

Which was sadly funny, because Aunt Sandy *usually* exaggerated.

Chapter Two

Knock. Pause. Louder knock. Pause. Bang.

"Aw, for crying out loud, Dinah, will you give it up already?"

"Cameron?" *Knock.*

Cameron thrust his head under the pillow, moaning. Kentucky was proving to be the most miserable retreat on Earth. "Go away!"

Bang. "Cameron Jacob Rollings, don't you talk to me like that, young man."

Cameron shot straight up. Nasty, shiny sunlight invaded his bedroom while the sickening smell of cinnamon assaulted his nose. "Aunt Sandy?" He hauled his protesting body up off the bed.

"What's gotten into you?" Sandy Burnside's unmistakable drawl came through the door. "Open up right now."

Cameron checked his watch as he shuffled to the door. It seemed way too bright to be seven-thirty. "Coming, coming." She swooped into the room the minute Cameron got the door open. "You have a key, Aunt Sandy, you could have just let yourself in instead of breaking down my door."

She poked a finger into her mass of blond hair as if to replace a stray strand. He always found that gesture odd on her—there was so much hairspray on that head he doubted gale force winds could pull a hair out of place. "I do not invade the privacy of my tenants. No matter how *rude* they are." She paused, taking in the strong scent of the room. "I haven't had a tenant in this apartment since Dinah moved in. Does the bakery send that powerful a smell up here all the time? I'll have a word with Dinah. Mac in the office downstairs has never complained about it before—of course, it is a nice smell at that. Not that you'll be here that long once your house is built."

Aunt Sandy's heels clacked into the kitchen as she poked her head here and there, assessing his meager attempts at unpacking his possessions—which were truly meager, considering he'd sold most of his New York apartment's furnishings before he moved and this apartment of his aunt's was only supposed to be temporary. "Honey," she pointed a red-lacquered fingernail at his oven, "y'all left that on."

Cameron stuffed his hands in his jeans pockets, leaned up against the refrigerator and glared at his aunt. "Dinah Hopkins."

"Dinah? What's Dinah got to do with your oven?"

Cameron reached for the coffeemaker. "Long story. Want a cup?"

Dinah closed her cash register drawer with a satisfied click. It was five minutes to nine and she'd made it through the morning rush—granted, with only two blueberry muffins to spare and a couple of last-minute substitutions for customers, but she'd made it. *Thank you, Jesus!* The oven repair company would open in five minutes and she could place a service call.

She'd never have made it without the use of Cameron Rollings's oven. She made a mental note to thank him sincerely—that is, if he ever spoke to her again. When that muffin pan had slipped off the counter and clattered loudly to the floor, he'd growled like a grizzly bear with murder in his eye. The man was from Manhattan; he should be used to all kinds of noise. Still, she had to give him credit; he had finally relented and let her use his oven—the third time she knocked on his door to ask. She'd whip up a batch of her famous macadamia nut cookies in an hour or so, after the sandwich bread finished baking, and take them over as a peace offering. He was her new landlord, after all.

And really, how had that happened? And so quickly? Granted, Sandy was the spontaneous type, but to sell the bakery out from underneath her (okay, so it was really just the space the bakery sat in—she still had her business) while she was gone on vacation? Without so much as a phone call to let her know? Sandy had come in the bakery just after eight, all flushed and apologetic, saying "If I'd known Cameron was gonna scare the pants off you in the middle of the night like that, I'd have left y'all a note or something."

There was a story behind Sandy's sudden sale to her nephew. Dinah was sure of that. She just wasn't sure whether she'd get the story out of Sandy or Cameron first.

He walked in the door about half an hour later—thick dark hair neatly combed, a yawn crossing his clean-shaven face. Cameron had the sleeves pushed up on the rust-colored wool sweater he wore over black jeans and his glasses were gone. With an expensive-looking watch and leather shoes, he looked everything and nothing like the man who had invaded her kitchen last night. He walked toward her with the shuffle of someone who hadn't gotten enough sleep.

"Good morning," she said cheerfully, as if she didn't feel a twinge of regret for imposing on her new neighbor and/or landlord so severely. "You've earned free coffee for the entire week."

"I'll need it." He yawned again. "Did you get a repairman to come out?" He didn't ask the question with a tone of concern—it was more defensive, as if confirming he'd have his kitchen to himself from here on in.

Dinah nodded and handed him a cup of her strongest brew. "He'll be here at eleven. I just hope it's an easy fix." She pointed over to a sideboard where she kept the cream and sugar in wildly colored ceramic jars, but he just took the cup and downed half of it right in front of her. Evidently the man took his coffee black and fast. Very New York.

"You and me both."

Dinah handed him one of the last two blueberry muffins. "Not to worry. Even if the oven's a goner, I can work through the evening using my own oven and get enough baked ahead of time to make it through another day. Can't say I'm looking forward to a week of baking twenty-four-seven if I have to replace it, though. Pastor Anderson might let me take over the church kitchen's two ovens if it looks like a long haul."

Cameron scratched his chin and got a thoughtful look on his face. "Anderson. Middleburg Community Church? Aunt Sandy's church?"

Dinah grinned. "Yep. So I guess that means I'll be seeing you Sunday mornings?"

"I suppose so," he said in a way that didn't let on if he found that good news or bad.

Never one to beat around the bush, Dinah opted for the direct approach. "You a churchgoin' man, Mr. Rollings?"

He chuckled and took another swig of coffee. "I still can't get used to that New Jersey-esque drawl."

"I have folks tell me it's endearing." Dinah lifted the towel off a batch of whole wheat dough that was rising on the shelf beside her. "A unique combination." She noticed he hadn't yet answered her question. The man's verbal dexterity told her he spent a lot of time in negotiations.

"Oh, unique is the word. I can tell you I've never heard anything like it ever before. How long have you been out here?"

"About a year and a half."

Rollings practically choked on his coffee. "That short?"

Are you saying I look old enough to have been here a decade? "I have a highly adaptive personality," she said defensively. "I can be at home in any situation."

"Or any kitchen." He reached into his pocket and removed a bottle of red sparkle nail polish, which he placed on her counter. "You left this on my kitchen table. Aunt Sandy had a field day when she found it. She didn't believe it was yours—she says redheads don't wear red."

Nobody told Dinah Hopkins what to do. She raised one leg and pointed to her toes, which were a delightfully sparkly crimson that matched the shade on the bottle. "It depends where." She snatched back the bottle of polish and tucked it behind the counter.

Cameron finished his coffee and tossed the paper cup

into the trash can by the door. "And by the way, yes, I am a churchgoin' man. Can't wait for Sunday, as a matter of fact. I gotta see what kind of church can handle you and Aunt Sandy in the same congregation." With the closest thing to a grin she'd seen out of him yet, he pulled open the door and headed off down the street.

"Well, well, I do declare," Dinah drawled as she put the Back in a Minute sign on her door and hoisted the tray of dough for a trip to the apartment oven. "What hath the Good Lord brought unto Middleburg?"

Cameron was beyond annoyed.

Served him right for buying a piece of property sight unseen. He, of all people, ought to know better. Then again, who'd have thought to not trust a family member? Aunt Sandy didn't seem to have a deceptive bone in her body. And in truth, she hadn't lied. It was good property.

She'd just left out a large chunk of the truth.

"The what?" A man in thick glasses had stared blankly at him when he went to town hall for the legal history of the Route 26 extension. The extension was the short street on which he'd purchased not only the land that would hold his new house, but three other eventual large-lot homes as well. A little bluegrass subdivision. His little corner of the world. A street to call his own.

A street that evidently didn't go by the perfectly normal name of Route 26. The perfectly legal, perfectly acceptable name of Route 26.

"That stretch out over by the Wentworths' farm?" the clerk had said. "You mean Lullaby Lane?"

"Pardon me?"

"Lullaby Lane. I can't remember the last person that

ever wanted to know anything about Lullaby Lane." He looked as if that query called Cameron's sense of good judgment into question.

Cameron pulled out his paperwork. "All my documents refer to that parcel of land as 'the Route 26 extension.'"

"Well, it is the Route 26 extension all right, but ain't nobody here ever called it that. It's been Lullaby Lane for as long as I've been here and I've been here a long time. All that property you bought is Lullaby Lane, mister, no matter what your piece of paper says."

Cameron immediately drove out to the land in question. He stopped his car in front of the rusted old street sign, leaning precariously to the right against a falling-down stone wall. His new empire, his future, was indeed Lullaby Lane.

Lord God, You're kidding. Lullaby Lane? Aunt Sandy and Uncle George sold me something called Lullaby Lane? I know land is land is land and it's only a detail, but could You just cut me a break here? It's salt in the wound, Lord. I used to be the smart guy at the office. Now I feel like the biggest fool in the county.

"She went through with it?" Dinah balked when Cameron returned to the bakery. "Sandy said George had an idea to finally sell Lullaby Lane by getting someone from out of town to invest in it by its legal name—the something-something extension. And it's *you.*" She got a look on her face that was half shock, half amusement. "You bought Lullaby Lane. Man, I thought *I* was having a bad week."

Cameron stared around the bakery. His bakery, actually. He now owned cupcakes and lullabies. It'd be hard to think of anything farther from real estate empires and high finance. "I bought a parcel of land called the Route 26 extension. The 'Lullaby' part was conveniently omitted."

Dinah hopped up on the counter and swung her legs over to slide off on the other side. "It's just a silly name. You look like the kind of guy who can handle a challenge like that. Oh, the oven's dead. Thanks for asking."

He stared at her. She was just this side of crazy.

"I reckon you'll be fine." She had a completely fake, completely unconvincing look on her face.

He glared until she dissolved into a cascade of giggles.

"Okay, okay, everyone knows it by Lullaby Lane. It's too sissy a name for all those horsemen and so nobody lives there."

He widened his stance. "Street names get changed all the time."

She shook her head, one unruly curl spilling out across her forehead. "Not in this town. Middleburg's as anti-change as it gets. You have no idea what you're dealing with here."

"You have no idea who you're dealing with *here*." He pointed to his chest. "I'll find a way."

She pulled some napkins out of a box and started stuffing them into a holder on a table. "Well, suit yourself, but that will take some serious leverage, and y'all only been here—what—two days?"

Cameron walked up and planted his hands on the table. "Well, then it's a good thing I'll have resourceful help." He looked her in the eye. "You can't afford a new oven, can you?"

"Well," she replied slowly, "I admit it's a bit of a cash flow challenge, but the money I was saving up to buy my building has surprisingly *freed up*." She gave him a pointed look.

So she had designs on owning the building. No wonder she'd bristled when he'd told her who he was. "Have you got enough to replace the oven?"

She stopped stuffing napkins, slowly moving her gaze up to meet his. "Almost."

He felt the first grin in days creep across his face. "I'll make you a deal. I'll loan you the money for the oven if you help me get my name change."

"It's just a name. You're getting all crazy over nothing."

"A sissy name according to you. As for the crazy, it sounds like I'll fit right in."

"I knew you would, honey," Aunt Sandy's voice came from behind him. He hadn't even heard the bakery door open. "I'm so glad to have you out here instead of squeezed into a stuffy suit back there in New York."

Cameron couldn't think of a moment when the word "impossible" didn't describe his Aunt Sandy. The one his mother called "loony Aunt Sandy." The "black sheep" sister of his mother's well-groomed Massachusetts family— although looking at the woman, "blond sheep" would have been a better metaphor. "Aunt Sandy, I'm thinking I should haul you in for fraud. And I know enough attorneys that I might just do it. Lullaby Lane?"

Sandy actually managed a look of remorse. "I did not lie. It is the Route 26 extension. That is its legal name. And I knew that my nephew Cameron was just the type of real estate mogul to take on a challenge like Lullaby Lane."

"A challenge is something you know about in advance and accept. As in willingly take on. This is more like an ambush. Dangerously close to a con job, if you ask me."

"Well, then," Aunt Sandy said with an indulgent grin, "I suppose I should thank the Good Lord I'm not askin'."

She pointed a pink fingernail at Cameron. "You just think about one thing, son. There's a reason you said yes. Maybe you know it somewhere inside, maybe only God knows it yet, but there's a reason a detail-focused, suit-wearin' planning type like you said yes to buying a hunk o' land sight unseen. You think about that, hon."

She sauntered out of the bakery as if that were an acceptable explanation. It was annoyingly true that what Sandy had done was legal, but it was not especially ethical in Cameron's book. And not at all the kind of stuff he'd expect out of a woman who claimed to have as much faith as Aunt Sandy did.

Cameron thought perhaps he should just point his BMW east—toward civilization—and start driving. Somewhere between here and the Atlantic Ocean, somebody needed a commercial real estate broker. God just wasn't cruel enough to make him stay here.

Chapter Three

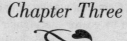

Dinah glanced up from her cookie dough while Cameron negotiated—again—with the oven man. At first she was glad to have Cameron offer to take care of dealing with the repair man—dashing between the bakery and her apartment oven all day was keeping her running—but the minute a dollar sign got involved the man couldn't seem to turn off the big city tycoon persona.

"You can't give me another fifty for the old one? You could get more than that for the scrap metal alone."

The repairman, a nice guy from a company that had been more than amiable to her in the past, looked up at Dinah as if to say *where'd you find this guy?* He pointed to a page on his clipboard. "I got a chart here says what I can give you. This is what I can give you. That's it."

Cameron looked up from the knob he was twisting. "No leeway?"

The poor man pushed his cap back on his head and exhaled. "Mister, if I had leeway I'd have given it to you the first time you asked. Asking three times ain't gonna make things any different, okay?"

"Okay." Cameron sounded as if he'd lost some kind of battle instead of gotten her one hundred dollars more than she expected for Old Ironsides. As a matter of fact, she hadn't even thought to ask them about buying the old one—she'd completely forgotten it could be sold as scrap. And that made a whole load of sense—the thing weighed a ton and she was pretty sure they sold scrap by the pound. Still, she thought Cameron was coming on a bit strong.

"Did you have to go for the jugular?" she asked the minute the repairman left to get his dolly out of his truck. "It's an oven, not a peace treaty."

"It's not the best deal until the other guy says 'no.'"

Dinah cut out another cookie. "He said 'no' twenty minutes ago."

"Reluctance is not refusal." Cameron pulled a towel off her counter and wiped the grease from his hands.

"Is that what you do for a living? Beat other people down until you get what you want? The real estate brokers on television are all smiling guys eager to help families find the home of their dreams. You, you look like you're going to snarl any second."

"My job is to get the best deal between buyer and seller. That's good for everyone."

"Okay, you're not the bad guy," she said, holding up her hand. "You're the good guy. But you have to admit," she looked straight at him, "you're mighty tightly strung for a good guy."

"You got your oven, didn't you?"

"Well, yeah, but I didn't need it to be the high-level negotiation you made it. I mean, I'm grateful, but you can take it down a notch here, okay?"

Cameron fiddled with the knob he'd removed from the

oven. Even though he had a game face that could scare those with weaker constitutions, Dinah could tell in his body language that he was giving in. Reminding himself to turn off—or at least tone down—the New York biz demeanor.

"Okay," he said after a pause.

She had to give him credit; he was still doing pretty good for a guy who'd uprooted himself and dived head-first into a whole new culture. She'd come here of her own free will (which somehow she knew he hadn't—or thought he hadn't), and it had still taken her a while to find her footing. The guy hadn't even been here half a week. As she loaded a second cookie sheet to take upstairs, Dinah said a quick prayer for rest and peace to visit Cameron Rollings—and maybe a little for herself, too.

The conversation lulled while the repairman and his buddy went through the huge task of getting the ancient oven out the bakery's back door. The thing was a behemoth—it astounded Dinah how big a space it left in the kitchen when they hauled it out. Installation of the new one would begin at nine o'clock tomorrow morning and after that, life might tilt back toward normal. Dinah hoped. Although part of her thought "normal" wasn't really on the radar anymore with Cameron Rollings next door.

"These are for you. Oven rent." Dinah appeared at his door thirty minutes later with a batch of macadamia nut white chocolate chip cookies. A stack of large, blueprint-like papers lay strewn out on his kitchen table. The display made it easy to picture him in the corner office of some Manhattan high-rise.

"Thanks," Cameron said, taking the cookies and putting them next to the papers. He had an elegant look about him that made him seem so foreign here, even in jeans. There was something in the set of his shoulders, the way he carried himself. A sleekness that came from always having the upper hand.

An upper hand she was pretty sure he felt he no longer had. That was pure intuition, but Dinah was a mighty intuitive gal and prided herself on her ability to read people. All that carefully crafted city confidence was coming unraveled in a few corners. She saw it in the way he'd overly defended his negotiation. In how he always tapped his left foot. There was a story there, all right. Even Sandy had alluded as much, although Dinah certainly had no idea what it was.

"I'm warning you," Dinah pointed to the cookies, "don't put those within easy reach. If you haven't eaten lunch, you're in trouble."

"I'll be fine," he said.

"Willpower is no match for the smell of my macadamia nut white chocolate chip cookies. Don't get cocky or I might come back up here to find you hiding an empty plate behind your back."

He didn't even laugh at the joke. "Baked goods don't scare me." He sat back down at the table, all business.

Dinah headed toward the door, but stopped before leaving. "So, why'd you leave New York, anyway?"

That made him look up. She knew it would. "To get away from people asking personal questions."

If he thought she'd be put off by a few snarky replies, he had a think or two coming. "No, really. What made you come all the way out here?"

Cameron pulled off his glasses and wiped his hands down his face. "Let's just say 'employment issues.'"

Dinah leaned against the open door. "You got canned?"

"Are you always this diplomatic?"

"I'll take that as a yes. I heard some famous guy say all truly innovative people get fired at least once in their careers."

"That's not true."

"How do you know?"

"Let's just say it was my lack of innovation that… heralded my job change."

"Meaning?"

He leaned on one elbow. "It was because I *wouldn't* get creative that I lost my job. And I didn't lose it, by the way," he corrected himself. "I merely agreed with the management that it would be best for all concerned if I left immediately."

"Honey, in this neck of the woods, that's called getting fired. Best own up to it now, so you can move on." She walked back into the apartment despite the dark look he gave her. "What kind of 'creative,' anyway? You mean cheating?"

"It has a nicer term in real estate. Alternative accounting. Although that's not the name I'd put to it. I wouldn't look the other way when some guy started skimming off the sales when apartment buildings were made into condos. Unfortunately that process has a lot of convenient little places to hide some cheating—if no one is looking. But I *was,* and when they started really putting the pressure on me, I had no choice but to go to the local authorities. I just couldn't sit by and watch them steal from people." He sighed and got up from the table. "But, as you can see, it didn't exactly go well for me."

Cameron had told himself over and over that he wouldn't go into his situation for his first couple of weeks in Kentucky. He had a set of polite but evasive answers for all questions about his sudden move, All of which left his skull in the presence of this relentless redhead. Why on earth was he getting into this with her? Already?

She blinked at him. "You're a whistle-blower?"

There had to be a more noble term for it than that. If only he could remember it. "Let's just say I'm a guy paying a very high price for doing the right thing at the wrong time."

She scratched her chin and he noticed it left a smear of flour on her cheek. Brown eyes were a very normal color—so why did they stand out on a redhead like that? And that red hair—did that come from God or a salon? He looked at her, standing in his kitchen with a bright pink potholder tucked into her back jean pocket, and thought there wasn't a single subtle thing about this woman. She narrowed her eyes and he wondered if he'd been staring too long. "Are you in the witness protection program or something?" she asked.

"Using my real name? Buying real estate? Here? With loudmouth Aunt Sandy?" There wasn't a more ridiculous notion in the world. Although, based on the last couple of days, perhaps a phone call to the FBI might be in order. Disappearing into thin air looked like an attractive option at the moment.

"Well, yeah, that'd hardly do the trick, would it?" she laughed. He expected her to have a high, musical laugh, but instead the low notes of her silky chuckle tickled him somewhere under his ribs. "But really, is that what happened? You called the cops on some guys so your own company fired you? Can they do that, legally? I mean, that's gangster stuff."

Cameron laughed. "My old boss would tell you that's simply a highly competitive marketplace. Everybody's scratching everyone else's back. Especially in a place like New York."

She shifted her weight. "Are you sorry you did it?" she asked in a tone so sincere it caught him off guard. "With all it cost you, would you do it again?"

Funny how no one had asked him that before now. Which was odd, because it really was the question of the hour, wasn't it? Was it all worth the cost? Would he have been able to sleep at night if he'd kept his mouth shut?

"You know," he said quite honestly, "I thought I'd know that for sure by now." Again, the prepared "noble guy" answer he'd crafted for the world just wouldn't come. "I keep waiting for that great big atta boy of peace to come down from God and, well, I'm still waiting."

A warm tone softened in her eyes. It looked far too much like pity and that sprouted a hard spot in the pit of his stomach. He really didn't know what he wanted from all this, but he knew for certain he *didn't* want pity. And for some reason, especially not from her. He shuffled his papers, suddenly wanting this conversation over.

"This isn't one of those black-and-white morality tales, Miss Hopkins. There's no hero, there's no wicked witch. I made the best choice I could at the time and I'll just deal with what comes."

Her face told him his tone had been sharper than he would have liked, but she seemed able to irk him with a single look. Not even his boss…*ahem,* his old boss—could get to him so quickly.

"Hey, you don't have to prove anything to me." She yanked the potholder from her pocket and huffed back toward the door. He slumped in his seat, half glad to be rid of her, half contrite for being such a beast.

"For what it's worth," he heard her call out from the hall as she pulled the door shut, "it sounds like you got a lousy deal."

When the door clicked shut behind her, he tossed his pencil down and thought, here or there?

Dinah stared at the envelope now opened on her bakery's kitchen counter. *Last time I checked, Lord, You were still in control. But can You see how I feel like the world's ganging up on me? Did she have to send this card? Now?*

A perfectly good morning—including the installation of Taste and See's new oven—had been ruined by a single piece of mail. All her euphoria over having an oven that actually obeyed the temperature she set on the dial— Dinah's math skills never really were up to speed when it came to compensating for Old Ironsides being 27 degrees too hot—was lost in the contents of one pale blue envelope.

Mom.

Dinah stared at the final two words of the card: "Come home." Suddenly she was eight years old and being told to come in from the thrilling Jersey seashore waves to wash up for dinner. To Dinah, "come home" never had any of those "welcome back" warm, fuzzy connotations. "Come home" was a command putting an end to anything fun or anything she called her own.

A command, in this particular instance, to "stop all this Kentucky nonsense and come back to your family where you belong." Dinah poured herself another cup of coffee and winced at the concept. She couldn't think of any place she felt like she belonged less than that manicured Jersey suburb. "All this Kentucky nonsense" felt more like "home" or "where she belonged" than anything on the East Coast.

Back home she was a square peg being continually squashed into a round hole. Here, those things her mother delicately called her "eccentricities" were welcomed, if not outright celebrated. Her craving to do something so pedestrian as baking, something so *manual* chafed at the academic and scientific values of her parents. Dinah knew God had brought her to Middleburg as sure as she knew anything in this world.

Middleburg is my home, Lord. How will I ever get her to understand that? Why can't she let me be who You made me to be? Why can't she let me be, period?

Dinah tucked the offending card into her back pocket as she heard the bakery's front door chime. She walked out of the kitchen to find Emily Montague coming into the bakery. The woman was grinning from ear to ear and it reminded Dinah of all the reasons she did what she did. She'd been looking forward to this appointment all week— how on earth could she have forgotten it was this morning? *Thanks, Lord, for sending me the reminder I needed,* Dinah prayed silently as she reached for the file of sketches she had ready for her friend.

"I'm here," Emily called out. "This is going to be so much fun."

Dinah motioned to the little corner table that sat by the bakery's front windows while she reached for a second mug and some hot water. "Tea for you, coffee for me."

Emily ran the West of Paris bath shop down the street and was in the middle of planning her February wedding to a local horse farmer named Gil Sorrent. Dinah was happy to see her friend so madly in love and even happier to bake her the wedding cake of her dreams. Even if it meant a little extra work around an already-busy time.

"You're sure you can do this? I just heard you'll be doing all the cookies for that new fund-raiser."

Dinah sat upright in her chair and hoisted her coffee mug. "That's right. You're looking at the Middleburg Community Fund's official Cookiegram baker. Complete with a fancy new oven thanks to the untimely but welcome death of Old Ironsides back there."

"Right," said Emily, "Sandy Burnside told me your oven died."

"I choose to believe God was simply better equipping me for the surge of business ahead. And no amount of cookies could put me off baking my friend's spectacular wedding cake." Dinah opened the file. "I took a look at the handkerchiefs you showed me and made a few sketches." Emily loved all things vintage and had given Dinah an assortment of delicate antique handkerchiefs with embroidered pastel borders as motifs to incorporate into the cake decoration. Emily was nothing if not a woman who knew what she wanted and Dinah liked her for that.

"You're sure you'll have time?" Emily was also a first-class control freak, although love had softened her edges.

"Honey, for you I'll make time. You're my top February priority. Cookies are easy. Wedding cakes—those are the stuff of bakers' dreams." All the more reason not to crawl back to New Jersey, Dinah thought as she poured Emily's tea. You've got a bustling bakery business to run.

They chatted through an hour of delightful options—fillings, shapes, colors, patterns—before choosing a design. Dinah was particularly tickled that Emily's favorite design was her first choice as well: a lovely, delicate trio of ovals—vintage enough to suit Emily's style, but not so fussy that her fiancé, Gil, would groan. They were a textbook case of opposites attract, those two. Emily was all soft, delicate pastels, whereas Gil was a large, dark, storm cloud of a man—at least before Emily came along. She couldn't be happier for the pair and baking for their wedding just made the joy that much more complete.

Wedding cakes were—and always had been—all the reasons why Dinah baked, wrapped up in one single confection. Why is it that no one in her family could understand baking's appeal for her? Why did they consider it some lower form of domestic servitude rather than the gift of beauty and pleasure that it was?

"So you want to tell me what's up?" Emily said as she closed the lace-covered notebook she used to hold her wedding notes. "Sandy told me she sold the building—your new landlord making you miserable?"

"Well, yes and no. Sorry, have I been that distracted?"

Emily smiled. "Just a bit. Come on, Dinah, what's up?"

It was no use hiding things from Emily. She was intuitive that way and they'd been good friends practically from Dinah's first day in Middleburg. "I got another card from my mom today."

Emily let out a little moan of understanding. "That's the third one, isn't it? She really is trying to patch things up between you."

Dinah pulled the card out from her pocket and slid it across to Emily. "Not that she was ever subtle before, but she's actually told me to come home in this one."

Emily quickly scanned the card and then looked up at Dinah. "Okay, but you don't have to go home. I can't remember you ever doing as you were told. You disregard Howard on a monthly basis for the fun of it."

Dinah served on the Middleburg Library board, vice

chair to Mayor Howard Epson, a man who believed himself
to be the most important person in Middleburg. A man who
loved issuing commands that Dinah loved ignoring. Still,
the two had managed a begrudging admiration for each
other which somehow got the job done. No one else had
ever lasted as long as vice chair of the library board under
Howard, and Howard was showing no signs of ever resign-
ing any of his many board chairmanships or from his long
run as Middleburg's mayor. "Ruffling Howard's feathers
is fun. Ruffling Mom's is playing with fire."

"She'll come around." Emily handed back the letter.
"Once she understands how happy you are out here, she'll
ease up. Parents want their children to be happy most of all."

Dinah sighed. "Yeah, but I can't help thinking something's up. Something bugs me about all her cards. Something I can't quite read between the lines yet. She's not
telling me everything."

"Maybe she's just afraid to admit how lonely she is
without you. Maybe it's easier for her to believe it's for
your own good to go back to New Jersey when she'd really
just like it for her own good."

Dinah drained her coffee and stuffed the card back into
her pocket. "You're probably right. She's been busier than a
beehive since Dad died, but she's never remarried. She says
she loves her independence, but that doesn't mean she isn't
lonely. Dad's been gone almost fifteen years now." She threw
Emily a look. "Maybe she's just itching for grandchildren and
has some dreamy neurosurgical student all lined up for me."

"Now that," Emily replied, finishing the last of her tea,
"sounds like a mother to me. You could do a lot worse than
a dreamy neurosurgeon. But you won't know unless you
talk to her."

Talk. Emily should know better than to make such a suggestion. There was no talking with Mom. Only listening to her version of how Dinah's life ought to be. A catalog of suggestions and disappointments in how Dinah chose to spend—Mom barely refrained from using the word "waste"—her fine young life.

"I think you are too smitten with farmer handsome to think clearly at the moment." Dinah stood up and planted her hands on her hips, diverting the conversation. "You do know the pair of you are probably the only people on the planet who could force me into pastels." She was a bridesmaid in the wedding, which sported the kind of pale green dresses Dinah would only tolerate for a dear friend. "The universe may shift on its axis to see me in pale mint and an actual ruffle. It could cause a crack in the space–time continuum or something."

Emily melted into the dreamy-eyed smirk of the soon-to-be-married. "I'll take that chance. Can you do lunch?"

Chapter Four

There had been days where Cameron craved this kind of solitude. Thirsted for a single uninterrupted hour. Now no phones rang. No one poked a head into his office with a "could you look this over?" interruption. They hadn't yet installed his cable or Internet connections, and the television only got something like four channels. He was stuck here at his dining room table, within the boring, empty confines of his apartment, facing a to-do list that rivaled only the slowest of weeks in Manhattan. So far he'd gone all five days of the new year without putting on a tie. This should feel like a grand vacation. Instead, the whole morning felt like an odd, unwanted sick day. Only he wasn't sick. He wasn't even tired.

What he really felt was an irrational irritation that no one barged through his door every hour to throw in a batch of muffins or poke at a cake pan. It had driven him bonkers while she'd done it, but now he missed the interruptions. As annoying as Dinah Hopkins was, she was the only Middleburg resident he knew other than Aunt Sandy and Uncle George—and he was in no hurry to talk to them at the moment.

It all begged the overwhelming question: What am I doing here?

Cameron almost breathed a sigh of relief when insistent knocking came at his door. He jumped up eagerly to answer it, but his face fell almost immediately.

"Wipe that scowl off your face, son, and go shave." His aunt Sandy's tone registered annoyance. Evidently he hadn't hid his disappointment very well. He'd never admit to anyone that he was hoping Dinah Hopkins was on the other side of that door, especially not to his big-haired blond relative.

Registering what she'd said, Cameron's hand flew to his chin—he'd forgotten to shave? That would have never happened in New York, even on his worst of days. "Um…why?"

"Because I'm not that bad a choice of company, and you're coming out to lunch. I'm introducing you around."

Starved as he was for human contact, that did not sound good. "'Around'?"

"You're goin' to Deacon's Grill for lunch." Aunt Sandy pushed past him to drape her leather coat across the back of his couch. "That's as good as meetin' everybody in Middleburg. Especially today, when the pies are all fresh. You'll have a dozen new friends by sundown."

"Won't that be swell?" he snapped sarcastically as he headed to the bathroom to find his cordless razor. There was no reason to be as irritated as he was, but he just couldn't seem to stop it.

Sandy followed him, pushing the bathroom door back open when he tried to shut it. She reached out and grabbed him by the ear like a schoolboy, having to stretch up to cover the foot between them even in her ridiculously high heels. For an absurd second he actually thought she was going to cuff him—and he probably deserved it. Instead, she pulled his forehead down to her height and kissed it. "I know you're hurtin', sugar. So I'll let that slide." She tugged his head a little, like a mama dog with a puppy by the scruff. It was a weird but completely disarming gesture. "I'm so proud of you for what you've done and all you've had to put up with. Y'all stood up for what was right just like your mama taught you. Don't think God wasn't watching every second."

How could the woman do that? Make you love her and hate her at the same time? Aunt Sandy was probably right—he needed to get out. He'd come here to launch his own business, to be the kind of resident broker Dinah had mentioned. The happy, straight-dealing kind. The sooner he re-planted himself in this strange little town, the better off he'd be. Find some new friends who didn't make his brain hurt. At least get a decent meal—the forty-eight-hour onslaught of baking smells gave him a nonstop appetite. If nothing else, this town seemed to have a full supply of great cooking—even if you couldn't get a single thing delivered.

By the time he finished shaving and changed into a nicer shirt, Aunt Sandy had sorted through the papers on his desk and rearranged the chairs around his dining room table. "There now, that's my handsome Cam. Put on your charm, hon, we're going to start the campaign today."

Cameron gulped. "What campaign?"

Sandy started fishing in her enormous handbag for something. "Why, to build your new business as a broker." She stopped and looked at him. "That's the idea here, isn't it?"

"Yes, but…"

She resumed her search, half her forearm hidden in the voluminous silver leather bag. "Well, sugar, nothin' in this town gets done quick or easy without Howard Epson on board. So today, we're puttin' a bug in Howard's ear about how wonderful you are and how he can help you. Ain't they ever taught you how to charm people back there in New York? What do they call it—'people skills'?"

It's a whole new brand of power lunch, Cameron thought to himself. "We do it just a bit differently. It's more predatory than charming."

Finally Aunt Sandy found whatever was eluding her at the bottom of her handbag. "Got it." She pulled out what looked like a crystal from a chandelier hanging on a little gold chain. She smiled and spun it in front of him. "Your housewarming present."

He raised an eyebrow. "A giant earring?"

She made a sound that could probably be described as a "Pshaw!" and headed toward his kitchen. "No, silly, it's a prism. You hang it in your window and it makes rainbows in the sunshine."

Cameron went to shoot her a disparaging look, but she was long gone. "Not exactly my decorating style," he called after her, but she was already sticking a pushpin into the window frame to hang the atrocity.

"Nonsense. Rainbows come after the rain. They're a symbol of God's promise. It's just what you need."

I'm going to die. The world's first overdose of charming. Cameron sighed. "You shouldn't have." He imbued the words with all the sarcasm he could manage.

"Don't say that. You're family." He ducked just in time to avoid the impending tweak she was about to give his cheek. "And I don't know what they're feeding you back in New York, but you could use some meat on those bones. C'mon, Cam, honey, we want to hit the lunch rush."

Lunch rush?

Lunch rush. The place was jam-packed. Cameron guessed this was the closest thing Middleburg saw to a crowd—which was only pleasantly bustling by Manhattan standards, to be sure. Aunt Sandy seemed to know everyone in the room and went from table to table introducing Cameron until he had so many names in his head that he wished he'd brought a pen and paper. Still, he recognized Howard holding court at the end of the counter and took the initiative to go say hello himself.

"Cameron, m'boy, good to see you again. I'm delighted Middleburg's caught the attention of a fine young entrepreneur such as yourself." Howard said it loudly and over his shoulder, so that the remark was addressed more to the room than to Cameron. Everything Aunt Sandy had said was starting to make sense.

"It's exciting to be in a town with so much potential," Cameron said, shaking Howard's hand. "Good character, good government," he leaned in and grinned, "good food, too."

"Sharp as a tack, Sandy," Howard called to Cameron's aunt as she came up behind him. "He'll go far."

Cameron slipped into a booth just to the left of Howard's crowd and eyed the menu. He must be as hungry as Sandy said; everything looked good. He ordered and tried to take mental notes as his aunt ticked down through the people in the room and how they'd eventually be connected to him through church, banking, real estate, even the library board, which she suggested Cameron get himself appointed to at the first opportunity.

"The library board?" Cameron balked, thinking it sounded unexciting. "You know, I'm not really the PTA type, Aunt Sandy."

"Well, I doubt you'd care for the Ladies' Mission Auxiliary. Library board's the best place to start. And Howard's chairman of the library board." She leaned in and lowered her voice, "Actually, Howard's chairman of everything. Just some of the other chairmen haven't figured it out yet." She emphasized her point by waving a breadstick, then caught sight of someone over Cameron's shoulder. "Here's another member of our library board now."

Cameron turned, expecting to find an unexciting librarian.

Instead, he found a certain intriguing baker. "Explaining town politics to our new citizen, Sandy?"

A shorter woman with honey-colored hair asked, "Is this your nephew?"

"It most certainly is. Emily Montague, meet Cameron Rollings."

Emily extended a hand. "Rumor has it you negotiate a mean oven deal."

He smirked. "My reputation precedes me."

"Nope," she replied, "Dinah just loves a good story. And she's probably just really glad to have a working oven again."

"I am," Dinah said. "Much as Old Ironsides lived a long and useful life, I'm glad to have an oven with a better sense of accuracy. There'll be no stopping me now."

"There'd better be no stopping you, Dinah," Howard cut in. "You're making all those cookies for the fund-raiser. We don't want to run out of Cookiegrams in our first year."

"Cookiegrams?" Cameron asked. It sounded too cute to be true.

"Cookie telegrams," Dinah explained. "To raise money for the Community Fund. It was Howard's idea."

Howard nodded.

"And you know, we need a few more bodies on the committee," Aunt Sandy said. Dinah, do you think we could find a job for Cameron?"

"We still need someone to get all the supplies donated," offered Emily. "That sounds like a negotiation to me."

Negotiating cookie supplies? Hardly the social introduction Cameron had in mind. "I don't know anyone in town yet."

"Nonsense," Howard called out. "You know me. And Emily, and Dinah and Sandy. That's all the start anyone needs."

Emily raised an eyebrow as she took a bite of her sandwich. "You didn't mention how handsome your new landlord was."

"Granted, he's cute in a suity, urban sort of way, but you know I'm not a fan of the suity urban type. If I'd have wanted to surround myself with upwardly mobile hunks, I'd have stayed back in Jersey."

"But the hunk's come to you. Divine intervention?"

Dinah put down her iced tea. "Let's list the reasons why that would be a bad idea, shall we?" She held up one finger. "He's my landlord now. I don't plan to change my 'never mix business with pleasure' mentality. Two," she held up a second finger, "you can take the man out of the suit, but you definitely can't take the suit out of that man. Look at him." She nodded in Cameron's direction, grabbing

Emily's arm when she actually started looking over her shoulder. "No, I don't mean really look at him. Figure of speech here?" She blew a curl out of her eye in exasperation—she didn't want to be having this conversation at all, much less with Emily's current love-struck outlook on life. "He's gonna last one year in this place, tops. The guy practically considers himself in exile out here."

Emily popped a potato chip into her mouth. "He goes to church, Dinah. And he negotiates a mean oven. And he loaned you the money to get it—you can't say that wasn't a nice thing to do."

"Again, mixing business with pleasure. Which brings me to reason number three: The guy's a tycoon in training. A predator in a three-piece suit. You should have seen him trying to get the last fifty dollars knocked off the purchase price. You'd have thought lives were at stake. No, I think I've seen enough to know he's not my kind of guy. The last thing I'm looking for is a guy who's got to go through life with the upper hand."

Emily smiled and selected another potato chip. "A girl could do worse."

Dinah mentally calculated the two months left until Emily was married off and her romantic energies could be trained elsewhere. Then again, it might get even worse once she was knee-deep in marital bliss.

Hadn't she fled New Jersey to get away from just this kind of thing?

Chapter Five

Cameron had never seen anything like this.

Well, actually he had, just under far more believable circumstances. He'd almost had to pinch himself to remind him that he was at the Middleburg town council meeting.

It wasn't the concept of a town council Cameron found strange. It was how seriously these people took their jobs. He'd seen less attention paid to civic ordinances in the city council chambers of New York. It was the oddest thing—no suits, no ties, no reporters and Emily Montague actually walked in carrying her papers in a basket (which nearly made Aunt Sandy's lime green iridescent tote look normal)—but deeply serious. Everyone had read all the materials sent to them in advance of the meeting—such conscientiousness might have made a few of his New York colleagues faint from surprise. No staffers spoon-feeding facts in this Town Hall.

They were talking about, of all things, the widening of a local road from one lane to two. A route that ran within a few blocks of "Cameronville" as he now called it in his head. Even though it sounded a bit too much like the infamous Pottersville from *It's a Wonderful Life,* it still was easier to swallow than Lullaby Lane.

Sure, the name change seemed a minor detail, but it set the tone for any future projects he'd have in this town. In this region. One day he'd need zoning variances, or streets widened, or sewers expanded, or permission for unattached three-car garages. Change. This name thing would set the pace for all his future expansions, lay a precedent for all the future changes he'd bring. It was vital. He had to win.

That meant stacking the deck in his favor. Last night, he'd conducted an Internet search of half a dozen Web sites and produced a long list of musical terms. No sense making this first change harder by bucking Middleburg's truly odd fascination with musical street names. But as one could expect from a town nearing the age of Middleburg, most of the good ones were taken.

So far, he'd come up with Fox Trot Lane, Tango Court, Cadenza Place, Prelude Circle and Sonata Avenue. Sure, most of them sounded more like they belonged on the billboards advertising ritzy suburban subdivisions he'd seen on tri-state turnpikes, but Cameron was too close to begging to be choosy. At this rate, anything that wasn't gooey-sweet and wasn't Lullaby Lane was on the table.

"Sidewalks?" Aunt Sandy asked peering above her sparkly reading glasses. "It costs that much to put in sidewalks? Aren't we spending enough puttin' in that second lane that we have to spring for sidewalks now?"

"Well," said "Mac" MacCarthy, "it's safer with the additional traffic. Kids walk to school along this route." He had his office in the space below Cameron's apartment and they'd had an intriguing conversation the other day about how Middleburg could be appropriately developed.

"All the more reason not to widen the road," said a rather crusty old man peering so closely at his papers that his nose practically touched the table. "Who needs more cars?"

"People drive cars," Gil Sorrent said wearily. Emily had introduced Cameron to Gil earlier this week, and Cameron had liked him instantly. "People who buy things and pay taxes and want to send their kids to good schools with adequate resources."

People who'll buy houses in Cameronville someday, Cameron rooted silently for Gil and Mac to succeed. They were trying—very hard—but from the looks of things, this road expansion plan had been on the table for months.

Great, Cameron thought to himself. I could be staring at Lullaby Lane until Labor Day. He was beginning to think his goal of locking in the name change by St. Patrick's Day was a bit optimistic. It was, after all, the first week of January. Give me a break. I wanted a faster start than this.

"Lots of our streets already have sidewalks, Monty," Emily addressed the crusty old man in a persuasive tone. "This isn't anything new."

"Well, it is expensive," the man said. "Expensive-*er* with those sidewalks. Seems to me, we wouldn't have to be putting in sidewalks if we wasn't putting in those lanes."

Cameron decided Cameronville would come with free sidewalks. And giant but tasteful signs that proclaimed "This isn't anything new." Well, except for the name. And the new houses. When did this get so complicated?

"Progress does cost money," Gil said tensely.

"May I remind you, Gil and Emily," Howard stated, "that one of you will have to step down off the council once you've married."

A woman Cameron recognized from the town library

immediately flipped open a massive notebook and began thumbing through pages. *"Spouses may not both serve on the council simultaneously,"* she read. "But we've never had council members marry while in office before." She looked up warmly at Emily. "It's rather sweet, if you ask me."

"You're all invited," Emily said with that dreamy tone of voice Cameron's cousin had used when discussing her impending wedding.

"You should come for the cake if nothing else," Dinah whispered over Cameron's shoulder. He'd been so intent on scouting out the town council that he hadn't even noticed her slip into the seat behind him. "It'll knock your socks off."

Cameron grinned and shook his head. He hadn't heard someone use that phrase since he was six.

Dinah leaned both elbows over the seat back beside him. "Hadn't even thought about the town council seat thing," she said quietly. "Man, that'll be a fight. Hope they don't ask my opinion. I like 'em both, but Emily's my pal. She's all about keeping things the way they are and Gil's all about progress. But really, they're Middleburg's biggest dilemma wrapped up in one adorable romance. Preservation versus progress. Look out, mister, you might have to choose sides."

"So, instead of asking 'Are you with the bride or the groom?' the ushers will ask 'Are you on the side of progress or preservation?'"

Dinah grinned. She had a wide, infectious smile to match those big brown eyes. "You're funny. But if I were you, I wouldn't mention that polling method to Mayor Epson."

I might as well be developing real estate on Mars, Cameron thought to himself. *This place is a whole other planet from New York.*

* * *

"Newcomer's curiosity for town politics?" Dinah asked him as they filed out of the town hall after the meeting.

Cameron stared at her. It was a look she was coming to recognize—a searching, analytical sort of stare that told her Middleburg and its citizens baffled him. The kind of look she'd give dough that wouldn't rise despite a perfect adherence to the recipe and ideal conditions. It was a full ten seconds before she realized he wasn't really staring at her; he was staring at her feet.

Oh, great, here we go again. As if a creative choice in footwear was the oddest thing this guy'd ever seen. Granted, it was cold, damp and January. The morning's rain had only barely avoided being slush and she had to pick her way around a frigid puddle or two, but it wasn't as if she'd sprouted a third arm or turned purple or anything. Certainly flip-flops in winter—however unconventional— didn't come near warranting the expression he bore.

"Aren't you cold?" he asked as he shifted his thick notebook to his other arm. He'd been taking notes all evening, but she hadn't been so brash as to lean over his shoulder far enough to read them. "I mean, aren't your feet cold?"

Now that was a rather laughable question, wasn't it? Dinah was an intelligent woman, perfectly capable of reaching into a bureau drawer and extracting a pair of socks should she find her feet cold. They were not in the farthest reaches of Africa—several very good clothing stores were within four blocks of her house. The answer to that question should be obvious. "I do own socks, you know. Several pairs. I even know what they're for. If my feet were cold, I'd put them on."

"How can your feet *not* be cold?" He looked around

them, as if the elements of the Kentucky winter would somehow back up his argument.

"How can you be so concerned with the state of my feet?" She pointed to the cashmere paisley monstrosity around his neck. It looked ridiculously stuffy with the casual navy pea coat he was wearing. "I could tell you I think your scarf makes about as much sense as my shoes, but some of us have better manners than that. Y'all must not put much stake in tolerance up there in New York." She threw the "y'all" in there just because the wince it produced in him was so much fun. The problem with this guy was that he was just so easy to tease. He seemed to come pre-loaded with irresistible things to make fun of—and he got so out of joint when she did.

Lord, remind me to go easy on him. I was once a newcomer, too, and look at the home You've given me here. It's not fair to pick on people when they're down, I know that. "Okay, the scarf's a bit fancy for this part of the world, but it's not so bad. And you still haven't told me why you went to the meeting."

"Reconnaissance."

Dinah stopped as they turned the corner onto Ballad Road and looked at him. "You been here all of—what? One week?—and already you're at war?"

"No." He looked annoyed, as if his combat-like behavior was perfectly normal. "I just like to know all I can about who I have to do business with. And not just town council, but half those people in there are on the zoning committee, right?"

Dinah ticked down the list of town council members in her head. "True."

"Those are the people I have to convince if I want to

rename Lullaby Lane, or change an ordinance, or do something so benign as put in sidewalks, evidently. I need to know the players."

It made sense. It was just the way he said it—all ferocious and mogul-like. Reconnaissance? Players? He acted as if there were some grand and omniscient moral principle at stake instead of one dumb old street name. One silly street name, granted, but Dinah would never put Lullaby Lane's name on a list of things worth so much time and energy. "So what do you do with your free time, Cameron? I mean when you're not studying for that test or scoping out the enemy?"

"You mean like hobbies?"

"I suppose. What did you do in New York when you weren't at work?"

The question seemed to catch him off guard, for his steps slowed. "I know what I wanted to do. I never did it, though. I was always at work. I worked all the time." His voice took on the tone of someone thinking out loud rather than having a conversation. "I mean, I went to church, I'd go out to dinner with friends and stuff, but that was just what I did in between working. Like sleep."

She'd seen loads of people like that back in New Jersey. People whose "off hours" were simply sleep bracketed by train rides in and out of Manhattan. The kind of people who did paperwork on their decks on Sunday afternoons or kept their cell phones right next to their dinner plates at restaurants. She supposed he hadn't even had cause to think of it before his life had ground to a halt and landed him in Middleburg. The slower pace of life was one of the things Dinah treasured about living here. You had time to be someone. Not just to *do something,* but to *be someone.* Time to ponder and hear God whisper in your ear.

"What did you want to do—you know, that you never got around to doing?" she asked.

"Play basketball," he answered without hesitation. "I wanted to be one of those guys who gets together at the city gym with his buddies every Saturday morning and shoots hoops."

Boy, that was sad. She expected something enormous and unattainable like climbing Mount Everest or photographing white tigers in Siberia. But hoops on Saturday mornings? That could happen. "That doesn't sound too hard," she said. "Especially now that you're here. I mean, this is Kentucky, where basketball is a very serious subject. Really, that's a low bar for life dreams."

Cameron shook his head and gave a half-hearted laugh. "Yeah, that's the worst of it. Not a high bar at all. And I couldn't even make it happen. Seems kind of sad now that I look at it. I was so busy getting ahead that there wasn't time for anything. College to MBA to job, all at full-out speed. I just realized yesterday that I kept a basketball in my New York apartment for three years and it's still in the box. I unpacked it yesterday, and the receipt was still in the bag with it." He hunched his shoulders against the evening chill and stuffed his hands in his pockets. "Three years and I didn't even find the time to take the thing out of the box."

There were times when Cameron seemed so angry with himself that Dinah thought he'd bubble up and boil over like a pot left on the stove too long. There was always something simmering just under the surface with him. Nothing she could ever put a finger on, just an inkling, but always there. "Balls come in boxes?" she asked with a mock fascination just as they were getting to the apartment building.

"The good ones do. I can see you know your b-ball."

She grinned at him. "It's that big orange thing that goes through the circle up off the ground, right?"

He laughed. It was the first time since he'd moved in that she heard him laugh. Granted, it wasn't much of a laugh— only a notch or two above the pathetic chuckle he'd given moments ago, but still an improvement.

"Go get it." On the list of potentially unwise suggestions, this one was at the top of Dinah's list, which did nothing to explain why it leaped out of her mouth. Maybe it was the way the regret darkened the corners of his eyes.

Or maybe it was the three varsity basketball letters stacked up in her high school yearbook.

He looked up in complete surprise. "What?"

"Well, this seems a pretty easy problem to fix. Get the thing out of its box and bring it down here. I'm not as good as I used to be, but since you've not touched a ball in three years, we ought to be even."

"As you 'used to be'?" He opened the door to the foyer shared by the two rowhouse-style buildings. "Is there something I ought to know? Besides," he pointed down at her flip-flops, "can you play in those things?"

There it was. The first spark of life in his voice. She kept wondering how the Cameron Rollings she'd met so far could take Manhattan markets by storm. There had to be more to him and for the first time, she saw a hint of it behind his eyes. The guy evidently had a competitive streak as wide as the Mississippi. The guy also didn't know she had a pair of socks and running shoes behind the counter in the bakery.

She stuck her key in the bakery door, applying a twang as she called over her shoulder, "Y'all telling me you're a'feared of a gal in rubber shoes?" Well, that was legal; sneakers are made of rubber, too.

His chuckle broadened out into a full laugh as he put his key in the door that led upstairs to his apartment. "Should I be?"

Dinah pointed at him as she pushed the bakery door open. "Unpack that ball and get down here in sixty seconds, mister."

Chapter Six

An hour later, Cameron was hunched over, bracing his weight on his knees as Dinah did a little victory dance around him.

"Three years on the varsity team," she admitted when she was up by a dozen points.

He should have known. "'The big orange thing that goes through the hoop?' Ha!"

Dinah dribbled and executed yet another perfect layup. "Well, would you have unboxed your ball if you knew I was any good?" The ball swooped through the chains that hung from the park basketball hoop, their chiming echo affirming her position.

"I've been whupped," he said, making a sorry attempt at a Kentucky drawl. "By a girl."

She palmed the ball against one curvy hip, her breath puffing white against the night air. "You've been bested by the 1999 regional collegiate champ left wing, that's all. Nothing to be ashamed of."

"Well…" he started to disagree.

Dinah smirked and bounced the ball back to him. "Besides,

now you've got time to practice. I'll be getting 'whupped' in no time. And then there's the little matter of the Middleburg Community Church men's basketball league."

"You've whupped them, too?" he moaned, enjoying the feeling of making jokes again.

"No, but you might. In a year or two. If you put your mind to it."

Cameron grabbed his jacket off the bench where he'd left it twenty minutes ago when play got decidedly serious. "I *knew* all I needed was a new life goal."

"Oh, I think you can aim a bit higher than that." She refastened the elastic that held all that wild red hair at bay. "But that's up to you and God and not necessarily my business."

Business. That was it, wasn't it? They were business associates. He didn't even know yet if she paid her rent on time. He checked his watch. "Don't you get up in…like…two hours?" It was past eleven. He felt completely exhausted, but it was a satisfying, spent tiredness rather than the stagnant exhaustion that had plagued him since leaving New York.

Dinah checked her own watch. "Five, actually."

He picked up her coat from where it had been lying next to his and handed it back to her. "Middleburg's sweet-tooth population can't be kept waiting." He spun the ball absentmindedly on a pair of fingers and turned toward the road.

"If you make any 'loafing around' jokes, I might be obliged to whup you again."

"If there is a next time, you'll play in flip-flops." He was her landlord. There should not be a next time, he thought to himself. "Tomorrow's the seventh," he said, even though it was an abrupt change in subject. They were back on Ballad Road now and it was a good idea to end this evening on a more formal note.

"Right," Dinah said, tucking both hands into her back pockets as she turned and walked backward to look at him. "Rent's due. Do I make the check out to you?"

"CJR Properties, actually." Dinah's rent check would be his first actual income for his new real estate development company.

"I'd guess that would be Cameron J. Rollings Properties? What's the *J* stand for?"

"Jacob."

"Good biblical middle name."

They'd reached the apartment door, and he was suddenly thankful her apartment was in the next building. He didn't like the idea of their standing in the hallway in front of their respective apartment doors saying good-night—that would feel just too weird.

"Good night, Cameron Jacob Rollings, promising real estate tycoon but paltry basketball star. Y'all sleep well and I'll bring the rent checks over in the morning."

Aunt Sandy had told him Dinah paid her apartment rent and the bakery rent with separate checks.

She hadn't told him he might have more trouble separating the tenant from the woman.

"Bible study? You don't waste a lot of time getting settled now, do you, Cameron?" Pastor Anderson seemed a bit surprised to see him the following morning. "You're more like your aunt than I thought."

"Well, Aunt Sandy can be…"

"Relax, son, we love Sandy here. She's a strong dose at times, I agree, but there isn't a woman who can get anything done faster in these parts than Sandy Burnside. She's got her fingers in a dozen different pies at any given moment and loves every minute of it. She'd be one of the first people I'd call in a crisis, that's for sure. Not much knocks that woman for a loop." He flipped through a large circular Rolodex, the kind Cameron hadn't seen on a desk in decades. "Now, it'll be the Thursday night one you'll want, right? You hardly strike me as the Tuesday night kind of guy."

Guys come in nights? he wondered. "I don't know. Who's on Tuesdays?"

Anderson made a dismissive gesture. "Oh, just a bunch of old coots like myself. George Burnside—that'd be Uncle George to you, I suppose, Vern from down at the hardware store, Howard Epson—oh, I bet you've met him by now, Monty Upshaw and Ted MacCarthy. You may have met Ted's son, Mac, he's more your age. Nobody under fifty. Hardly your crowd."

Nobody under fifty, but two of the members of the town council. "Oh, don't be so sure." Not that Cameron chose his Bible studies for professional advancement, but he needed to get to know these people and right now he'd had his fill of young urban professionals. He didn't need social connections from his Bible study; he needed wise counsel. Odd as he might have found it two months ago, a handful of seasoned, Godly men sounded like just the ticket for his current state. Besides, Aunt Sandy had already threatened to fix him up with endless clusters of "you young people."

Pastor Anderson raised a surprised eyebrow. "Us old coots? Really?"

"Pastor Anderson, I've had my life turned inside out, upside down, and moved halfway across the country. What I need from a Bible study is good advice, the voice of experience, and—quite frankly—someone who can't beat

me at basketball. Being a 'coot' sounds perfect. If you'll
have me, that is."

"You're sure?"

He was. Cameron had that grounded feeling in the pit of
his stomach that he usually got in the middle of a good
decision. And it was refreshing to make a good decision that
didn't cost him loads of anything. And really, Howard wasn't
as bad as everyone made him out to be. He was enthusiastic, rather self-promoting, but he was downright humble
next to some of Cameron's former colleagues. Somehow,
and for some unknown reason, Cameron liked Howard. He
had a good relationship with his own father and had always
been comfortable around older people. This seemed like
the perfect choice, even though Pastor Anderson looked at
him like he'd asked to join the Women's Guild.

"Yes, sir."

Anderson smiled. "Now cut that out. If you're going to
be MCC's first ever 'young coot,' we'd best get on a first-
name basis right this minute." The blond, balding man
held out his hand and grinned. "I'm Dave. Save the 'pastor'
title for formal occasions, okay?"

"Fine by me."

They said their goodbyes, and "Pastor Dave"—as Cameron
decided he'd call him just for the time being—handed him
a copy of the Bible study the men were using and a schedule
of which chapters were covered on which nights. Finally,
something to put on his calendar. Sixteen dates and seven
phone numbers had never felt more precious. As he walked
home from the church—a whopping eight-minute stroll—
Cameron had to stop and stand in wonder.

Whatever would the commerce wizards back East think
of this "young coot" now?

* * *

Bang.

Mumble, mumble, *bang!* Cameron looked up from the place where he was sweeping snow off the building's back stairs late that afternoon. Another aggravated moan, followed by the unmistakable sound of breaking glass, wafted out into the darkening air. He looked over and noticed Dinah's back door was open—it often was, even in winter, to help let the baking heat out of the kitchen. Based on the sounds escaping through the door, all was far from well at Taste and See. Cameron propped the broom against his railing and wandered down to the bakery's rear entrance.

Dinah was crouched over a dustpan, trying to clean up glass shards while sucking two fingers on one hand. Her shoulders heaved in frustration—she was either about to cry or was crying already. *No, Lord, you know I'm not good at this kind of thing.* Good or not, he was here and Dinah was bleeding if not worse. Only a coldhearted goon would turn around and walk away. Taking a deep breath, Cameron poked his head through the doorway. "Hey, you okay in there?"

Dinah turned her back quickly, but a telltale sniffle escaped her as she dumped the shards into the wastebasket. "I dropped something."

Cameron leaned against the doorframe. "From what I heard, you threw something. Some*things.* Sounded like some first-class Kentucky fit-pitching down here—not that I'd know or anything."

She turned to look at him, her face more embarrassed than angry. He'd never seen her look like that. Something—or someone—had hurt her badly. The sight of her forlorn and red-rimmed eyes made his chest tighten up.

"We pitch fits in New York, too, you know," he offered, looking for a bit of brightness to return to her eyes but finding none. He ventured a few steps into the kitchen, picking up a baking pan that lay near the door. It had a large dent in one corner. "I think we call it 'wigging out' or something less colorful, but the sentiment's the same." He set the pan gently on the counter between them. "Lousy is lousy all over the world."

"I'm fine." She straightened her back and he recognized the defiance of the supremely wounded. He'd barked the same two words to dozens of people as he carried his box of possessions out of the office not too long ago.

Cameron saw a broken wooden spoon on the counter where he'd set the pan and picked it up. "Somehow I gather this is a bit bigger than a burned loaf of cinnamon bread."

"Yeah," she said, unsteadily. She plucked a dish towel from the oven handle behind her and dared to dab at her eyes. "Just a bit." Something in his heart tugged him toward her, pulled by her desperate attempt to stand straight. He was somehow keenly aware that she probably would have sobbed and thrown more things had he not arrived. Usually he avoided such emotional scenes, but he might be capable of some compassionate diversion. "Is there any coffee left out front?" The bakery closed a while ago, but maybe she hadn't emptied the big self-serve carafes yet.

She nodded, shifting her weight, and he noticed some papers hastily stuffed into the back pocket of her jeans. Had she just gotten some very nasty news? "How about I go pour us a couple of cups? I think we both could use a break."

"Sure." She sniffed again and pointed to the small collection of ceramic mugs lining her back counter. "I'll just finish up in here."

She needed a moment alone to collect herself. He wasn't sure how he knew—it wasn't like he had sisters or a long string of girlfriends on which to base his intuition. He just recognized a kindred spirit in someone else who didn't like to get caught feeling out of control. Sometimes you can get yourself just enough back together as long as nobody has to watch. Like the human resources official who, even though he had been ordered to stand over Cameron as he emptied out his desk, simply said that he'd wait outside. It was such a subtle act of kindness—to leave a man one shred of dignity before he was paraded out of the building with half the division watching.

She had fixed her hair when he came back into the kitchen with two cups of coffee. Her face was still blotchy and it looked as if she'd splashed water on it. Two more baking pans—each with dents—sat lined up next to their wounded companion on the counter. Cameron set down the coffee cups and pointed at the largest of the trio of pans, now pushed out of shape into almost a triangle. "Good arm. Ever thought about a company softball team?"

She didn't laugh, but one corner of her mouth turned up slightly. "I'm more the basketball type, remember?"

He picked up the pan, admiring it from different angles. Whatever was on that paper in her pocket, it had made her good and mad. "Want to talk about it?"

She sighed and took a long drink of coffee. "Not really."

He sat down on the stool, admittedly relieved. "Okay."

A minute went by. She put her coffee down. "That's it? Okay?"

Cameron looked up at her, puzzled.

"No negotiating, no argument, no trying to pull it out

of me, or words of concern—just 'okay'? Where do you guys learn this stuff?"

Cameron sat very still for a moment, wondering what in the world had just happened. He had thought he was doing really well. Cameron realized his attempt at diversion had just veered off into the realm of the emotional landmine.

"Do I *look* okay?" She flung her arms wide. "Do I look like I'm all fine and I don't need to talk about it? Like I don't need to try to make sense of the master of emotional blackmail I call my mother?"

Oh boy. Go slow. Big trouble ahead. "No," he said very carefully, "you don't look okay."

She pushed her coffee away and stood up. "Who could be okay after the letter I just got? I mean, really, what human being could possibly be calm after something like this?" She began walking around the kitchen, opening and closing cabinet doors, shifting containers.

Cameron wrapped his hands around his coffee mug. He prayed for protection like a man going into battle. *Cover me, Lord, I'm going in.* He tried not to let her see the deep breath he took before saying, "What kind of something?"

He figured she would whip the letter out of her pocket. He didn't suspect she would slam it down onto the counter with the force that she did. He grabbed both their coffees before they spilled. "'Come home,' she writes. Of course, she's been writing 'come home' since Christmas, and I knew something was up. I just couldn't figure out what. So now she pulls out the big guns. 'Come home because I'm dying' qualifies as a really big gun to me. Why didn't she tell me earlier? In person? Maybe use a *phone?* Who dumps that kind of news in a letter? That's the kind of conversation you have face-to-face with people you love, right? The kind of stuff you share before you get to the dying part. She didn't even tell me she was sick. How can you not talk to someone for a year and then tell them this?"

Cameron knew, just by the way she rushed her words, that her anger was there to hold her fear in check. "Maybe that's why she wants you to come home. So you can talk about it."

"Oh, no," she refuted, fiddling with a pitcher that had a collection of wooden spoons in it. "That kind of 'come home' I could maybe handle. This is the bigger kind of 'come home.' This is *move home*. Stop this silly Kentucky nonsense and come back…" her voice caught for a moment. She was backed into a corner of two counters, looking trapped and scared. He took a step toward her.

She stiffened. "I love it here," she said defensively. While her voice screamed for help, her eyes told him to come no farther.

He stilled. "I can see that."

"But she's sick. Really sick. What if she's really… She needs me." Dinah hugged her arms across her chest. "I love her—sort of. Well, I know I do. I mean, you always love your mother, right? Even when you don't. We make each other so nuts, we can't understand each other, but I love her. And I love it here. This place is so much my home now. Would God make me choose between the two?"

If there were ever a question that Cameron Rollings should be qualified to answer, it would be that one. He'd asked it of himself enough times. God had made him choose between the career he loved and the principles he held. But he hadn't any wisdom to offer on the subject. He still didn't have any idea what the point was of such "no win" situations. Why choose between two painful consequences when all it really got you was the pain of both?

"I don't know, Dinah." It was the first time he'd spoken her name.

"It's lousy, isn't it?" she said, shifting her weight as her eyes roamed around the room. She was trying not to lose it. "I mean, the timing is so awful. Just now when everything's picking up here. She's young. She's healthy. She can't be sick. She's so bad at all that medical stuff—it'll scare her to…" She swallowed the unfortunate end of that phrase and gripped the counter on either side of her as she leaned back against it. "I'm not a heartless beast, you know. I know she's desperate and panicked. Anyone would be." She was gulping in the words and the tears threatening behind them.

He took one careful step toward her, watching her reaction. She was backed up against the far side of the room as it was. When she didn't flinch, he took another small step.

"Life just knocks it out of you sometimes. It's lousy, and it's not fair, and I could think of a few other New York adjectives I'll skip. You got any good Kentucky ones for something like this?"

She took a deep breath. "Eddie Matthews down at the garage could probably string a few colorful phrases together to fit the situation." He took another step toward her, watching her fingers loosen their white-knuckle grip on the counter. "That boy swears like a sailor."

"We had a guy like that in our office. Gutter mouth. The day they fired me, some part of me wished I had access to that kind of vocabulary just for the day. You know, a one-day leave of absence from clean Christian language kind of thing. So I could say ugly words to match an ugly situation."

Cameron was near enough to put a hand on her shoulder

now, and his heart twisted at the tight knot he found there. The touch undid her—he knew it would—and she sagged into him as she lost her battle with the tears. "I thought you said you weren't fired," she said while crying on his shoulder.

He forced himself to wrap his arms around her, finding it all too easy to do once he'd started. "I thought you said you didn't need to talk about it."

Chapter Seven

"He's right. This isn't the kind of thing you can work out on the phone. You need to go out there."

Janet Bishop sat on Dinah's couch as they talked through the current dilemma a few days later. Having come home from college quite a few years back to help her mom run Bishop Hardware and care for her ailing dad, Janet was both a sympathetic ear and the voice of experience.

"Part of me doesn't want to go," Dinah moaned, sinking into the couch. "I know it's not Mom's fault—she didn't choose to be sick—but how come this *feels* like emotional blackmail?"

Janet tucked one foot up underneath her. "I think it's perfectly natural to feel blindsided. You two don't have the best relationship. Usually, you start with something small, like 'call me on Sundays' and work your way up to 'see me through cancer.' This came out of the blue for you."

"But you did it," Dinah said, meeting her friend's gaze. "I can't believe you're even letting me talk like this. I must sound so…selfish, so disrespectful to you."

"You're a bit of a renegade." Janet gave a lopsided smile.

"Disrespectful sort of comes with the territory. Conciliatory isn't the word that comes to mind when I think of Dinah Hopkins, you know."

Dinah narrowed her eyes. "Great. Are you about to tell me God's got a character overhaul in the works? That's your guy in the overhaul business, girlfriend, not me." Janet had met Drew Downing when his renovation television show came to repair MCC's preschool from storm damage. Janet was the reason Drew was still here—they'd fallen hook, line and sinker for each other. The Ballad Road Bachelorettes, as Dinah used to think of herself and her two single shopkeeper friends, were becoming an extinct species.

"You could think of this as a recipe. You're adding a new ingredient to your life."

Dinah shot her a look. Metaphorical thinking wasn't helping. "You came home when you were needed."

"Yes, I left school to help run the store. But you have to remember, my relationship with my parents was a bit…warmer than yours. And I have to say, I was asked very gently if I wouldn't mind taking a year off school. I didn't get a letter out of nowhere demanding I 'stop this nonsense and come home.'" She pointed to the letter in question, now sitting on the coffee table between them. "That letter's a piece of work. I can't say I blame you for thinking you're walking into a storm."

Dinah reached out and touched the letter. "She's sick. She's scared. Who handles things well when they're sick and scared?"

Janet stood up. "Which is exactly why you should go see her. Take a few days for everyone to make sense of things. You know, if she realizes you're not going to ignore her, maybe she won't get quite so demanding. You might find a compromise."

Dinah stood as well, picking up the two coffee mugs and the letter off the table. She walked with Janet to the kitchen. "You don't know Patty Hopkins. She doesn't do compromise."

"You know," Janet said as she pulled Dinah into a big hug, "I used to think the same thing of you."

Dinah teared up and hugged her back hard. Janet had become such a good friend here in Middleburg. Dinah had lots of good friends here. She had a life far richer than the one she'd known in New Jersey and the thought of leaving it to go deal with a traumatized, demanding cancer patient made her almost ill herself. "I just hate it when friends love you enough to be honest," she moaned into Janet's shoulder. "The nerve."

"What?" Janet pulled back to look at her, blinking back a tear or two herself. "Don't they have nerve in Jersey?"

Dinah sighed and opened the door for her dear friend. "Maybe I better go see." *Oh, Lord, I'm so afraid if I set foot in New Jersey I'll never be able to come back here. This is my home, Lord. Don't make me leave it.*

"Any prayer requests?" Pastor Dave asked, wrapping up Cameron's first meeting with the Old Coots' Bible Study. Make that the MCC Tuesday Night Men's Bible Study. Cameron was so afraid if he didn't stop thinking of them as the Old Coots, he'd call one of them just that to his face. They might laugh and enjoy it—after all, they'd called him the Young Coot four times already tonight. Then again, they might not.

"I'd like prayers for my upcoming exams," Cameron said.

"I'm pretty sure I'll do fine, but it'd make my life much more complicated if I botched these and had to wait longer to get my real estate license transferred to Kentucky." He watched as a few of them wrote it down on the index cards Pastor Dave had passed out. These guys took their prayers seriously. He liked that. With his church friends from back in New York, "I'll pray for you" was always meant with good intentions, but didn't always result in actual prayers. And he was as guilty of it as the next guy. "And I think we should pray for Dinah Hopkins and her mom."

"I heard," Vern said sadly. "Tough going. Janet told me those two weren't close before and that kind of stuff's hard enough as it is. I love Dinah's goodies, but she don't strike me as the nursemaid type."

"Yeah," said Howard, nodding. "I'll miss those sticky buns while she's gone. And I am concerned about the impact on our Cookiegrams. It's a serious setback."

Only Howard could see hampered Cookiegrams as a serious setback compared with a life-threatening illness. "I'm sure a day or two with the bakery closed won't be that bad." Cameron hadn't even thought about Dinah having to close the shop.

"I'll talk to Janet." Vern scratched his chin. "Maybe she and Emily can pull something together. Emily's kind of busy with the wedding and all, but I'm sure they'll make time."

"I'd lend a hand, but I've got inventory this month, and you wouldn't believe the work that makes these days." "We're heading down to see the grandkids for two weeks." "The Kentucky Mayor's Conference has some very serious issues to deal with this year." And on it went as the men, half of whom were retired, began a litany of how busy each of them were. Cameron thought most of them

wouldn't last one afternoon on his former schedule—
"busy" here was a walk in the park by New York standards. Still, he had youth on his side. But none of that
made him feel any better when all eyes turned to him. It
became obvious he had a schedule too empty to gripe about
with this crowd. Cameron watched Howard draw a breath
and while he saw it coming, he knew there wasn't a single
thing he could do about it.

"I bet you don't have to know squat about baking to
supervise a bunch of volunteer bakers, Cameron. A few
phone calls with your persuasive skills and we'll keep
Dinah's bakery up and running in her absence. It'd be the
Christian thing to do and you'd get to know more folks in
town, too."

"I…" Cameron felt he ought to at least attempt a defense.

"Nonsense, m'boy. Phone up your aunt, pull Janet and
Emily in on the deal and you'll have it covered by sundown."
Howard's beefy hand came down on Cameron's shoulder
like a stockade. "Unless you got better things to do with
your time."

Cameron's mom used to complain about how she got
roped into volunteering for things down at church all the
time. He never understood it. How hard is it for one intelligent woman to say "no" to an unreasonable request?

He understood it now.

"I'm sorry, Mom," Cameron repented aloud in the
hallway as he raised his hand to knock on Dinah's door.
Yes, this could have waited until morning at the bakery. But
it was only eight-thirty (Pastor Dave wasn't kidding about
the Men's Bible Study's "early bird special" meeting hours
never going much past eight) and this was rather like a dive

in a cold pool—best to get it over with right away and start swimming. And honestly, he wanted an excuse to see Dinah's apartment. After all, she'd seen his. He told himself this was about parity, but some part of him already knew this was more about curiosity than equity of information.

She came to the door with her hair down. He hadn't realized until just this moment that he'd always seen it pinned up. It was slightly wet, as if she'd been in the shower earlier, and it framed her face in various shades of red waves. Drier locks escaped into orangish wisps—the kind she was always blowing out of her eyes. Other locks still hung in damp, darker twists close to her neck. He had the oddly poetic thought that the hair was like the woman—complex, complicated and always changing. Cameron wasn't sure how many seconds went by before he said, "Hi. How are things?"

Her expression was as complicated as her appearance. "Okay, sort of." She leaned against the doorway—she did that a lot, he noticed—but he couldn't be sure if it was a nice-to-see-you casualness or a oh-great-you-again kind of impatience. "Trying to sort stuff out, I suppose."

"Got a minute?"

She looked surprised, perhaps a bit wary. "Sure, come in." He recognized the tense undertone as the same one his staff had used when making small talk. The constant awareness that for all the niceness, the pecking order hadn't disappeared. He was her landlord, after all. And now, essentially a creditor as well, because they'd made the arrangement for the oven payment. A guy with a history of negotiation success should be more comfortable with holding all the cards, but he was unnerved. He needed to tread carefully here, for he was about to deepen the inequity and she wouldn't take to it well.

She didn't. "Absolutely not!" she cried when he'd finished presenting his proposal. She pushed back from her kitchen table—a big wooden slab of a thing painted a riot of bright colors. "I can't accept that kind of help."

"Why not?" He knew she'd balk first; she had to talk out her resistance before she'd even consider the idea.

"Because it's way too much. Closing for two days won't put me under." She stood up. "I hope you think better of my business skills than to assume I'd cut things that close to the bone. I've got a cushion." She turned and began poking around her kitchen, which was just as much a storm of color and texture as everything else. Artisan pots stood next to art deco resale shop-ish containers. Beaded curtains framed kitchen windowsills filled with a collection of what looked like cheesy souvenir salt-and-pepper shakers. Next to the stove stood stoneware urns with bouquets of every kitchen utensil he'd ever seen—and some he'd never seen. It felt more like an artist's studio than a kitchen. Which, knowing her, made sense.

Cameron chose to say nothing and let her talk more. After half a minute of reordering a row of glass-and-copper containers on her counter, she turned to face him. "Besides, I haven't even decided if I'm going."

Actually, she had; he could see it in her body language. Her fierce independent streak was just still fighting it. "You should go," he said as gently as he knew how. "This will just make things easier."

Dinah looked at him for a moment and he wondered if his tone of voice had surprised her. She hiked herself up to sit on the counter, her turquoise flip-flops kicking toward him. The sparkles in them matched the design of the studs around her jeans pockets. Despite an effort not to notice, he hadn't seen the same pair twice in his two-week residency in Middleburg. Maybe she really did have three dozen pairs of the things.

"Exactly how," she leaned toward him, running the tip of one finger down the chrome edge of the counter beside her, "will having a horde of volunteer do-gooders invade my kitchen make things *easier?*"

If his tone had surprised her, her tone now did the same to him. The edge bit just as intensely as her tirade in the kitchen the other night, only darker. *Please, Lord, I'm in way over my head here.* He drew guidance from his only reference: negotiation. Cameron was somehow aware that he was in this prickly situation because of his negotiating skills. And he knew—with what Aunt Sandy would have surely called intuition—that God placed him here to negotiate Dinah's acceptance. He had the skills to get her to say "yes," even if this had nothing to do with real estate. Purposely mirroring her body language, he leaned in, his elbows on his knees so that his face was below hers. One key to successful negotiation was to get the resistant party to reframe the situation.

"Well, now, you can't look at this like charity." He looked up at her, watching her eyes narrow slightly at that word. His instincts were right. Dinah was like Aunt Sandy—Uncle George always said she'd help anyone out, but you had to practically hog-tie her to accept any help for herself. "You need to look at this as marketing."

Dinah leaned back and crossed one knee over the other. "Marketing?"

"Middleburg citizens just love to get into each other's business. They love to help out, meddle, all that small-town stuff. People will come in to buy things while you're gone just because it's helping out. It's sort of a twisted-up bake sale. Your friends will take care of your shop. Your loyal customers will come in and buy twice as much just to lend a hand. You'll get new customers who'll come back to see how much better your own baking is when you return. You'll become the talk of the town even before this Cookiegram thing starts. You couldn't buy this kind of publicity. Everybody wins."

"You really think," Dinah jumped down off the counter, "that I believe one word of that? That's the biggest load of…"

"Howard will love me if I pull it off," Cameron interrupted, having saved his trump card for last.

"What?"

"This was his idea. Well, I think it was actually Vern's, but you know Howard. They decided we should help you out and that I should head it up." Cameron stood up and took a step or two toward the counter. The room smelled of cinnamon and something exotically floral. He had saved the remark about Howard's favor as a way to convince her, to make her feel as if she were helping him out instead of the other way around, but the moment he said it he suspected it to be a deeper truth—that he really did just want to help. "But Howard's right. It is a good idea. This is your mom and even if things are all mucked up between you two, I think you should go. And I think it would be great if it didn't cost you customers and income to do it." He picked up the pink potholder lying on the kitchen table and fiddled with it awkwardly, needing something to do with his hands.

Dinah didn't say anything. "Look," he went on, somehow thinking more words would help, "I don't know half these people, but I do know you've said this is your home. People want to help you out. Howard may just want his cookies, but everybody else just wants to be nice. This may be a once-in-a-lifetime kind of thing—I know I've never seen anything like it—so I say go for it."

"You've never seen people being nice before? You mean New York really is as bad as everybody says?" Under the veneer of humor, her face showed a storm of emotion. Cameron understood, at that moment, that the liability of leaving the business was the one last defense she had against making the trip to see her mother. And he had just offered to remove it. It took the conversation past uncomfortable, too far into personal, as if he were stealing his way into a moment where he didn't belong.

"So it's your business opinion that I should go?" She circled around the kitchen to end up wedged into one corner, just as she had that night at the bakery.

"It is."

"And personally, you think it's a good idea."

"Yeah, actually, I do."

"Well, I don't have to listen to your advice, now do I? I mean, you've got no authority over me, even if you are my landlord."

She'd never accept this as someone's advice, this had to be her decision. A move she had to own entirely. He could see that. "Dinah, you don't have to listen to a word I say. You can do whatever you want and no one can judge you for it. It's your family, your bakery, your life." He held her eyes for as long as he dared. "But I'll help if you want me to. We all will."

The word "we" sunk a single, tiny root in his heart and held fast. He'd used it without thinking, felt it without meaning to. He pulled his eyes away from hers, off-balanced and startled.

"Okay," she said quietly.

"Okay," he repeated, unable to say more.

He bumbled his way out of the apartment as quickly as courtesy would allow, feeling disturbed and exposed. He got all the way back to his own apartment and had been sitting there a full ten minutes before he realized he still had the pink potholder in his hand.

Chapter Eight

Dial the seven.

Dinah had dialed the other ten numbers of her mother's phone number but couldn't seem to make her finger push the final button. It should be such an easy thing. People phone their mothers every day. People *ought* to phone their mothers. Well, yeah, but not after almost two years of "radio silence." *Hey, Lord, could You extend me a little grace and let me get her voicemail?* Even if she did, Dinah knew that would be as much cheating as she had accused her mother of—cowardly delivering dire news in letter form instead of picking up the phone. Go girl, be the bigger woman here. Dial the seven.

Letting out something close to a yelp, she did. And listened, breathless.

"Hello?"

"Mom?" It wasn't really a word. More of a gulp. *Oh, Lord, this is so much harder than I thought it'd be. Save me!*

There was an excruciating silence on the other end of the phone. "Dinah? Dinah is that you?" The relief in her mother's voice wound its way around Dinah's heart and squeezed tight.

"You got anyone else calling you 'Mom' these days?"

It was a dumb crack, but Dinah thought if she didn't make a joke she'd start crying on the spot. She hadn't counted on the sound of her mother's voice to do her in so fast. Not after all the bad blood between them.

"No." And that was really the whole point, wasn't it? They had only each other. She heard her mother pull in a halting breath on the other end of the line. "Just you."

"How are you?"

"Well, it hasn't been the best year in memory. I'm…I'm here, and I suppose that's all that matters." The *for now* went unspoken.

It should be easy to communicate, but somehow the words "I'm coming" tangled up in the back of Dinah's throat. "I'm going to catch a flight Sunday. Come out for a few days so we can figure this out."

"Come out." So Mom noticed Dinah hadn't said *come home*. "For a few days." Her mother's disappointment was so obvious Dinah could practically reach through the phone line and touch it. This is what made her nuts about their relationship—there was no give and take at all. Either Dinah did everything her mother wanted or she was an utter disappointment. Come on now, Dinah, you knew this wouldn't go smoothly. Stick it out. She's sick and she's scared. That'd make anybody difficult. More difficult.

Dinah made a fist and then released it, choosing that action over the long, loud sigh she'd rather have made in reply. "Sunday to Thursday. The weekend is busy at the bakery. This will give us time to talk over what's going on."

"What's going on," her mother said sharply, "is that I'm dying." There it was, the melodrama that made Mom so hard to deal with, that made it so hard to figure out what was true and what was exaggeration.

"You didn't give me any details. Or say how long this has been going on. Help me, Mom, give me more to go on."

"What more does a daughter need? I'm dying. How can I tell you more when you won't talk to me?"

"I'm talking…. I'm *trying* to talk now. Let's just try and get through this first part without biting each other's heads off. What is your diagnosis?"

"I told you, it's cancer. You know it runs in the family."

Every disease known to man "ran in the family," according to Dinah's mother. "I know you said that, but there are lots of *kinds* of cancer, Mom. What kind do you have?"

"The kind where you die at the end. What does it matter which body part it starts with?"

Dinah closed her eyes and counted to three. "It matters. Help me out, Mom. Just tell me some of the details."

"You never wanted to know them before. How many times did I write you? How many since Christmas—the Christmas you weren't here? My last Christmas. You weren't here for my last Christmas."

Can you guess why? Dinah thought. "I don't think this is helping. I'm coming for a few days. That's a good thing. Let's just take it from there, okay? It's going to be hard enough as it is."

"It's hard. Yes, it's hard." Oddly enough, that had given them something to agree on. Her mother's voice softened a bit. "You're coming this Sunday, are you?"

"Yes. Listen, can you get an appointment with your doctor Monday? So we can both get more details?" It had been Janet's suggestion and a wise one. "It would help me a lot to be able to talk with him. Do you think he would see us on short notice?"

"He's good. He cares. He'll see us."

Dinah couldn't remember the last time she'd used a word like "us" to describe her mother and herself. "Vs." was a little bit closer—they seemed able to argue about everything. How would they make this work? People needed calm when they were sick, not the nonstop battle going on between her mother and her. "That's good. You should feel like your doctor cares about you."

"I should feel like *you* care about me."

"I'm coming in for a few days, aren't I?"

"I had to beg you. My own daughter and I had to beg."

"No, you just had to be honest with me and tell me what was going on. Can we not get into this? Look, I know now and I'm glad you told me and I'm doing my best to be there as fast as I can." Dinah switched to something more practical. "You don't have to have Uncle Mike pick me up at the airport. I'll just get a cab, okay?"

"He'd be thrilled to see you."

"I know, but a cab will be fine."

"Dinah?"

"Yes, Mom?"

"I'll be thrilled to see you. I'm…well, it's hard."

There it was, the soft voice that cut through all the arguments, all the difficult behavior. They really did love each other, somewhere under all that expectation, defiance and disappointment. Maybe they could get back to that, even if just for a little while. The lump in Dinah's throat tugged at her words. "I know, Mom. I'm coming." She did it again—stopped short of saying "I'm coming home." A gap of silence stretched out between them.

"I love you." Mom was on the edge of tears. Dinah wasn't far behind.

"I love you, too, Mom. We just have to figure out how not to hate each other so much in the process."

Her mom gave a weak laugh. "Yeah, we do, don't we? Think we know how?"

"God only knows." And that wasn't a figure of speech. Dinah was pretty sure God was the only one who knew how to get them through whatever was ahead.

Cameron stood with Howard Epson at the head of Lullaby Lane and stared. This road would someday be his neighborhood. There had been a house here once, an un-remarkable farmhouse and barn sitting on perhaps a dozen acres of horse pasture. Remnants of the typical black plank fence lay scattered across the grass like fallen twigs. The spot was a clearing of flat land surrounded by the rolling hills that still amazed Cameron—they looked so much like something out of a movie, all wintry and rural with horses feeding as though staged for a tourism commercial. Won-derfully old trees, thick-trunked and broad, stood sentry here and there. A few would have to go to make room for the construction, but most would be able to stay and witness the rebirth Cameron had planned.

The land was ready. It was a goofy sensation—some-thing urgent and inexplicable. It was the flip side of the calling he'd felt to turn his coworkers in to the authorities after he'd realized the extent of corruption in his office. That was a dark, burning, Ezekiel-esque roaring of the bones that threatened to overtake him if he didn't finally cry out despite the consequences. Which had been dire, as he knew they would be.

This was closer to an insistent child, tugging on his sleeve with an impatient yearn to grow up. The land wanted to be what it hadn't yet been allowed to be. What, Cameron hoped, God was planning for it to be.

"You feel it?" Howard said, rocking back on his heels and tucking his hands into his coat pockets.

The question startled Cameron. He wasn't yet ready to talk about the sensations going through his head as he looked at this land. It was just a little too weird. "Feel it?"

"I walk, early in the morning, through town. There's only a few people up that early downtown—farmers might be up, but they're out a ways from Ballad Road. I walk down the street and ask God to show me what the town needs. Not necessarily the people—although I care about them, too—but the town itself. I ask Him to show me the long view. The bigger picture. I think God calls men like us to see those things."

Cameron stared at the man and found himself feeling a little leery of sharing any deep civic connection with Howard Epson.

"I know it sounds pompous, son. And I know what most people think of my motivations for staying on as mayor for all the years I have. Truth is I'm just doing what God and Middleburg ask me to."

What God and Middleburg ask me to. Wasn't that essentially what he was feeling? It was at once comforting and disturbing to hear his gut feeling explained by the likes of Howard Epson. Cameron couldn't think of a better reply than, "I guess."

"It's good land, Cameron. It just lacks someone listening to what it needs."

"I think it needs a name change." Cameron had planned to be so much more subtle about it. To slowly bring Howard and the committee around to his way of thinking like Aunt Sandy advised.

Howard paused for a long time before saying, "Can't say as I'm particularly fond of that idea."

"It's a tiny detail and you've already seen how it's set back the sales of this place. It's not worth it. Some changes are good."

Howard shook his head. "I know you think it's a trivial matter, son, but Middleburg's reluctance to change is part of its strength. We've lit our Christmas tree on the first Wednesday in December since 1910. Our church door has been blue for seventy-five years. There's a whole world banging on our doorstep to change and too much of it," he looked at Cameron, "is just for change's sake. We hang on to the small things because it helps us hang on to the big things."

"Well, Howard, when I listen to what the land says it needs, that's what I hear." He couldn't believe he was admitting this aloud.

Howard glanced up at him, the hint of a wink in his eye. At that moment, he looked not so much the boisterous old mayor as he did an amused grandfather. "So you *are* listening. Hmm. Let's walk around," said Howard, buttoning up his coat. "Let's see what else God has to say."

And so they did. Cameron and Howard walked the land for a good twenty minutes. The conversation never returned to its initial philosophical level. As a matter of fact, it became mostly a list of Howard's Cookiegram requirements peppered with the occasional remark about this shrub or that fence. Hardly the "listening" Cameron was expecting. Howard informed Cameron, during their wanderings, that he was raising the Cookiegram fund-raiser goal to $15,000.

"Do you really think it can raise $15,000? That's a lot of money and you've never done it before." Not only was it a lot of money, it was a whole lot of cookies. Did Dinah realize she was about to become a cookie factory? On top of everything else she was dealing with at the moment?

"Can't miss," Howard said with a confidence Cameron certainly didn't share. "No reason not to—it's the kind of thing everyone can get involved in, it's a good cause and really, who doesn't like cookies?"

"Well," Cameron said as he pushed the leaning Lullaby Lane sign back up to a vertical position, "everyone likes cookies, but not everyone's ready to pay a fund-raiser price to get them. Even Dinah's." The moment he took his hand away from the post, the street sign slumped back into its sad tilt. "See?" he ventured, throwing Howard a sideways glance, "that says 'I want a new name' to me."

"Funny," Howard replied. "Sounds more like 'go get some concrete' to me."

At that moment, it struck Cameron that he liked Howard. Who'd have ever thought such a thing possible?

Chapter Nine

❧

"*How* much?" Janet looked shocked.

Dinah sat back in her chair. She, Janet and Emily were discussing Cookiegram details after church when Dinah informed them of the new goal Howard had set for the fund-raiser. "You heard me. $15,000."

"Did he bother to find out what anyone else thought of this?" Emily asked.

Janet and Dinah just stared at Emily as if to say "What do you think?"

"This is Howard," Dinah said sharply. "Consensus isn't in his vocabulary. He put it in the paper this morning. Told me *after* he gave his son the news." Howard's son Peter was a reporter for the local paper and Howard had been known to make extensive use of that connection.

"Just because he told the paper doesn't make it true. That's a high number. Wouldn't we be better off setting a lower goal and exceeding it than setting one that'll be so hard to pull off?" Janet was already punching numbers into her calculator. "That's a thousand boxes of cookies,

Dinah. Middleburg's only got four thousand people. And we haven't even deducted our costs yet."

"Even if we get supplies donated," Emily suggested, "we're still going to need all the help we can get."

"*You're* going to need all the help *you* can get," Janet said. "You can't make…" she punched a few more buttons, "five hundred dozen cookies the week of the fund-raiser. You're going to have to make some ahead of time and freeze them or something."

"My wedding cake…" Emily said, slightly panicked.

"Is still my top priority, honey. Your wedding's more than a week after the Cookiegram thing—that's more than enough time. You can't make a cake ahead of time like you can cookies, anyhow." Dinah reached out and grabbed Emily's hand. "Don't you worry about that cake one bit. It will be lovely and it will be there." Dinah turned to Janet. "I've already thought about the logistics of making all the cookies, even before this exploded into Howard's personal cookie triumph. I've been collecting recipes that freeze well before and after baking. If we have any problem, it'll be finding enough freezer space to hold all those cookies."

"Gil has a big freezer out on the farm. I bet we could use that," Emily chimed in.

"Gina's got to have one down at the Grill, too," Janet added. "Maybe we can find someone else to donate use of their big freezer." After a moment, she shook her head. "$15,000. Where'd he come up with such a pie-in-the-sky number like that anyway?"

"You know," Dinah replied, "I asked him that and he said the oddest thing."

"What'd he say?" Janet put her calculator back in her handbag.

Dinah leaned in on her elbows and stared at her friends. "He said to ask Cameron Rollings."

"How on earth should I know?" Cameron asked as Dinah burst into his apartment. The woman barely waited for him to open the door—she just waltzed in the moment he turned the knob. Rather like Aunt Sandy. He did have an idea what Howard meant, but he sure wasn't going to have any conversations about "listening to God's plan for the town" with Dinah Hopkins.

Dinah spun on her heels. Cameron wasn't quite sure how she pulled off the maneuver in flip-flops. "Why would he say something like that unless he felt you could tell me?"

"He's an enigmatic, mysterious old coot?"

"He's *Howard,*" Dinah shot back. "Get real."

"He's not so bad. A little self-absorbed, but essentially he's a good guy."

Dinah stilled, staring at Cameron as if he'd just declared the sky green. "Howard? They've done something to you in that Bible Study. This is Howard Epson we're talking about. Pompous. Unreasonable. Imperial."

"Imperial?"

"I'm sure he thinks he's king. He's certainly not heading a democracy."

"I'll admit his vision can be a bit off-kilter, but…"

"'Can be?'"

"Essentially, there's a good guy under all that grand-standing."

"Howard Epson? You're taking Howard Epson's side?"

Cameron reached into his fridge for a bottle of Ale-8.

Vern had introduced him to the local soft drink at their last "Coots" Bible Study meeting and Cameron was hooked. "There are sides?"

Dinah leaned against the counter. "You know what I mean."

Cameron held a bottle out to her, but she made a face—obviously, it wasn't her favorite. "Look, I know it's a really high number and I would have chosen something a little more realistic, but who knows? Maybe Middleburg will step up to the plate and we'll all be thanking Howard for his boldness."

"Oh, Howard has boldness in spades, you can be sure of that. But I ain't been thankful for it yet," she fired up her trademark artificial twang, "and I'm not fixing to start anytime soon."

Cameron changed the subject. "I looked over the table you drew up." He'd asked her for a detailed task schedule for the days he'd be organizing the bakery staff. He'd had another conversation with Howard about the wisdom of putting a clueless New York broker in charge of a Kentucky bakery, but Howard insisted. Aunt Sandy had started compiling a list of volunteers, but the roster was already filled with confidence-busting commentary such as "not good with money" and "foggy before noon" beside many of the names. *I used to manage a staff of eleven. I can handle forty-eight hours of baking,* he'd told himself. *I don't even have to bake, just supervise.* Cameron had handed the list back to his aunt, asking her to add to it—preferably people with actual baking skills and the ability to be coherent at dawn.

"Thanks, by the way." Dinah's eyes were on her feet.

"You're welcome. It makes for a good study break from all this boring exam stuff, anyways."

"Liar," she said, half a smirk creeping across her face as she brought her eyes up to meet his. "But thanks anyways."

"Howard doesn't like the idea of changing Lullaby Lane, you know. I'll expect your full lobbying support as payback. I'm going to have to change that man's mind."

"Now who's setting a sky-high goal?" she asked, feeling the playfulness return to her voice.

"Shouldn't you be packing?"

Of course she should be packing. But packing meant getting ready to go see her mom and the last thing she was at this moment was ready to see her mom. It was so much easier to worry about the bakery than to contemplate the emotional roller coaster that was to come. "It'll take me five minutes to pack," she lied. She'd actually packed—and unpacked and repacked—four times already. What, exactly, does one wear to confront one's maternal mortality? Which color goes best with oncology and intergenerational trauma?

Dinah's mother was forever pushing "tasteful" clothing on her, hinting with those subtle looks and occasionally devastating comments that she ought to "tone things down a notch." One of her favorites was "go for a more effortless look," which Dinah found hysterical. Shouldn't a woman put some effort into her looks? To Dinah, effortless was sweatpants and no makeup. The kind of thing you wear on your couch watching romantic comedies the week you break up with your boyfriend. The look best accessorized by a pint of Extreme Peanut Butter Fudge Chunk.

No, what Mom really meant to say was "stop trying so hard to stand out," because to Mom, "standing out" meant "getting desperate for a man." And really, the only "desperate" in this duo of a family was Mom's thinly veiled desperation for grandchildren and a son-in-law whose résumé played well at dinner parties. And now Dinah was venturing home to see if it was humanly possible to love this woman through chemotherapy. Or worse. Who wouldn't rather worry about whether three members of the choir's alto section could pull off four batches of sticky buns?

Suddenly, Cameron's hand was waving in front of her face. "Dinah!"

She flushed. "Sorry, wandered off there for a moment. I'm just a little stressed, you know?"

He put down the papers. "Would you like to go humiliate me in basketball? Might work off the nerves." He ran a hand through his hair, which Dinah noticed was just starting to grow out of its precise office cut. The ends flipped up just a tiny bit behind his ears, miniscule rebellions to the neat edges of the style. It made her wonder if it would wave if he grew it longer. Would his beard be darker or lighter than his hair if he grew one? The vision of clean-cut Cameron Rollings with tangled hair and stubble simply would not materialize in her head—as if his hair was incapable of that kind of mutiny. Had he been a radical as a teen? Or one of those scrubbed-faced, clean-cut golf caddy types?

"No," she replied, not liking where that train of thought led. "I really should pack. Look, are you sure you want to take this on? You don't know half these people and my ticket is nonrefundable, but everything can be negotiated and—"

Cameron put his hand over her mouth, silencing her. The contact was obviously meant to be a joke, a tussle between friends, but it startled her. They hadn't touched since he held her when she broke down that other night, the night of Mom's letter. Even then, she'd pulled back as soon as she could bear to stand upright on her own. His touch was more difficult to bear somehow; it seemed to make her feel as though she owed him something. Which was ridiculous because Dinah touched people all the time—too much, in fact. She hugged customers, wrapped an arm around anyone from church and blew kisses to everyone at Christmas.

Cameron was different. Touch didn't come to him as naturally or as casually, which made it valuable and even safeguarded somehow. Now with his hand touching her face, it was as if something far too intimate had shown up far too early.

He pulled his hand away, as if embarrassed by the impulse, replacing it instead with an awkward pat on her shoulder. His eyes told her this was the best he could manage under the circumstances. The most he would allow himself. And probably the most she should allow him.

"Hey," he almost stuttered, "it's going to be fine. You're going to be fine. You're strong enough to do this."

He'd given voice to her deepest fear. "No," she gulped out, "I don't think I am." She didn't like what his voice did to her. "Besides," she said, stepping away from him, "how on Earth would you know, anyway? You haven't been around long enough to see the real Dinah Hopkins. It's all just bravado, you know. Smoke and mirrors. Tricks with frosting and sprinkles."

"Yeah," he said, "You're right. You often see damsels in distress whacking ovens, threatening them in the middle of the night, giving unsuspecting brokers a pounding on the basketball court. You, Dinah Hopkins, are no cupcake. You're a whole lot of something, but no cupcake. If you'll excuse the bakery metaphor."

"Use 'em all the time." She smirked. "Handy, those

baking metaphors." They were grasping for a dignified way out of this conversation.

Whatever connection strung between them a moment ago had faded into an embarrassed discomfort, but not without a lingering echo of warmth. "I'll remember that," he said a bit stiffly, as if trying too hard. "When I'm manning the fort, surrounded by the MCC women's choir."

Chapter Ten

Dinah had played this moment over in her head so many times it was difficult to believe it was actually happening. Difficult to believe the key that she could never bring herself to take off her keychain was now in the lock that opened Mom's door. Or, given their year of estrangement, should she knock? She felt a surge of guilt over the incredibly preventable chasm now yawning between her mother and herself—it should never have had to be this way. This couldn't be how God designed mothers and daughters to make their way through the world. And yet, Dinah and her mother somehow seemed powerless to stop the cycle of annoyance, irritation and misunderstanding between them. Again she waffled: Open the door with her key like a member of the family, or knock like the guest she'd become?

She was still standing there, holding the tarnished gold key in her hand, when the door swung open and removed the question entirely. Mom.

And yet, not Mom. The face before her held the bones and eyes of the mom of Dinah's memory, but the skin and hair of a weary, weaker woman. An unwell woman's sunken cheeks and an older woman's frail, spotted hands. As if she'd aged a dozen years in the time since they last stood arguing in the driveway, when Dinah had driven away with the sting of angry tears in her eyes. It had been no way to leave. There had been no way but to leave. Dinah had left not only to find her own identity away from her mother's expectations, but in hopes that distance might allow them to relate again one day. She'd once planned this reunion so differently—coming home the victorious entrepreneur, the well-adjusted daughter returning on her own terms.

"Well, hello there, Bug." Even her mother's voice sounded frayed around the edges. One thin-skinned, blue-veined hand clung to the open door. The rings her mother always wore seemed to dangle loosely on her fingers, her perfect nail polish an odd counterpoint to the unhealthy pallor of her hands. It seemed a decade since anyone had called Dinah "Bug." Back when she was small, her dad used to joke about her enormous brown eyes, saying she could stare at him "like a bug." She used to hate it.

She didn't today. Her heart seemed to ball up in her throat behind the single word, "Mom."

All the reasons Dinah left home were still there, still festering. Yet, in the space of that single exchange, they deflated. Lost their force—even if only for that moment—behind a wave of love and compassion that Dinah was surprised to find still there.

Dinah shrugged, unable to leave the moment gaping between them like that. She tugged her suitcase into the house, taking in the oh-so-familiar setting. The outdated, fussy doilies on the back of the couch—the ones she used to steal and turn into wedding gowns for her dolls. The collection of china angels in the curio cabinet. The way Mom propped up her throw pillows in pairs at either end of the sofa. There were changes in the detail—more angels, new pillows—but the house still felt the same. As if she could walk to the upstairs linen closet and still know where to find the guest towels.

Mom's hands stayed splayed against her chest until Dinah slid her suitcase against the living room wall, but then she reached out to cup Dinah's face. Had Mom lost that much height in one year? It wasn't possible that Dinah had grown, was it? When her mother's cool fingers pressed against her cheeks, Dinah choked back a surprising sob of emotion. Frail. She looks frail. Everything looks frail. *Oh, Lord Jesus, this is so much harder than I expected.*

"You've changed your hair." Tears tugged at the edges of Mom's words as she ran her hands along Dinah's bangs. Dinah hadn't remembered that she'd cut it into layers last fall. She flinched, unconsciously steeling herself for the surely critical assessment of that choice. "It's different."

That was big. To anyone else, the neutral statement might have proven a disappointment. Neutrality, however, was foreign territory to Mom. "Different," without the accompanying sharp tone Dinah would have expected, was almost a compliment. Almost. Different meant "you've changed and I'm going to try not to hate it." Well, in as much as you could read that complex emotion into one hairstyle comment. It's a start.

They went out to a Sunday night dinner and fumbled through the rest of the evening, reaching for an ease that never quite came. Everything felt just slightly out of whack, which surprised Dinah, even though it couldn't really be different under the circumstances. It bothered her how much her old bedroom felt like a guest room. Which was foolish, considering she hadn't lived at home in half a dozen years. It had all the "empty nest" trappings—new drapes, pullout couch, desk, optimistic but little-used craft supplies…craft supplies? Since when does Mom do the scrapbook thing?

As she took off her dinner clothes and slipped into jeans and a sweatshirt, Dinah grimaced at her brown suede shoes. Why'd I wear those? she wondered. She'd been so sure that the deep-seated urge to fit in had long been silenced. Pulling a pair of flip-flops out of her suitcase felt like sticking her tongue out, but she did it anyway. Shaking herself, she went downstairs to the kitchen table to have the conversation they had been avoiding all evening.

Mom had updated the kitchen here and there, nothing extensive but always the neat, conservative style Dinah associated with her mother. What stuck out most were the prescription bottles that now served as the kitchen table centerpiece. They were arranged—if you could call such a thing an arrangement—in a fabric-lined basket. As if encasing them in beauty hid the evidence. It was a very nice, expensive-looking basket, with all sorts of sections for organizing, one of which held one of those gigantic multiday pill sorters. The kind old people used.

Mom was old.

Of course Mom was old. All mothers were old, even when they weren't. Dinah thought her mom was old when she was in the first grade, when Mom was the ripe old vintage of twenty-eight—one year older than Dinah was now.

Fifty wasn't old. Or shouldn't be. Fifty should be a big birthday party and a long-postponed trip to Europe. Arthritis, retirement, reading glasses, but not…not "I'm dying, so come home."

It had been easy to dismiss Mom's letters as theatrics on paper, as the seeds of truth but not the full truth. Dinah did expect her mom to be unwell. But Mom looked gravely ill.

Dinah sat down and both of them wrapped their hands around the charming stoneware mugs of tea Mom had set out. Both of them tried not to stare at the medicines. The big ol' elephant was in the room, lumbering now—as it had through the afternoon and at the restaurant—with stomps as loud as the present, yawning gap in conversation. Start. Just start.

"So…what is it?" Dinah didn't look up.

Her mom produced one of those here-we-go sighs. "I already told you, it's cancer." She pulled the pill sorter out and began filling the next day the way she might deal a hand of bridge.

"Can you be more specific?" Why was she making this so hard?

Her mother's hand stilled and she looked up for just a moment—an icy flick of a glance. "Lymphoma. Does it matter?"

Dinah counted to ten before saying, "It helps to have more to go on. I'm trying to process this."

Mom snapped the Morning section shut and started in on the Noon section. "It's not complicated. You can't re-arrange the details and come out with a different ending, Bug. I'm…it's not a recipe you can adapt."

Mom's nod to Dinah's profession wasn't complimentary. "You…well, it's just that you're so…resigned."

No fewer than six pills went into the section before Mom snapped it shut. "I don't really have a choice now, do I?"

Dinah rose up off her chair to pace the kitchen. "Of course you do. Medicine is changing all the time. There could be new treatments, alternative medicines—have you even gotten a second opinion on this?"

Mom sat back in her chair. "The chemo didn't work." With an exasperated look on her face, she tugged one side of her hair. Dinah watched in horror as her mother's entire scalp seemed to move. That wasn't a questionable gray-hiding dye job, it was a wig. "Want to see?"

It was almost cruel, the way her mother was throwing this at her, wielding the shock of it as if it were a weapon. Had it been anything but her own mother's illness, Dinah would have been even more appalled at the treatment she was receiving. But really, can you call someone out for how they're handling their life-threatening illness? Knock them for their post-chemo manners? Post-unsuccessful chemo? "For crying out loud, Mom, you've *had chemo?* Didn't you think I *ought to know?*"

"Don't you go there with me. Don't you put this on me, young lady. I'm not the one who up and left. I'm not the one who didn't come home over the summer, or Thanksgiving, or Christmas. It's not like you don't know the address. Or the phone number." Dinah heard the carefully controlled catch in her mother's voice. "I will not beg for attention from my only daughter."

Dinah rolled her eyes. "Don't you think this is a little bit different? Isn't this above and beyond the family squabble stage?"

"No," came her mother's clipped reply. "I don't think this is the slightest bit different. Do you think I enjoy knowing that pity and death were the only way I could get your attention?" Dinah hated how easily the word "death" rolled off her mother's tongue. "Do you think this has been a lark for me, with your father already gone? *Alone?*" Her voice rose on that last word, taking on a shrill edge. Patty sat very still for a moment, her knuckles white against the dark wood of the table, and then she went back to filling the Evening section of the pillbox. The thing must have held almost two dozen pills by now; Dinah felt the sheer volume of them as if they'd piled up in the back of her throat.

She slumped back down into the kitchen chair. This was so impossibly, exasperatingly hard. "Are you…" she pursed her lips and wiped her hands on the thighs of her jeans, struggling to get the words out. "Are you really… you know…dying?"

Well, yes, it was sort of an insulting question, but no one in this room was trying to be nice anymore and it had to be asked. There was so much drama that facts were the only stronghold she could find.

"You think I'm inventing this?"

"You just sound so sure you've exhausted all your options. I mean, come on, Mom, you're only fifty."

"Thanks for the 'only.'"

"Mom…"

"Facts? You want facts? Yes, Dinah, I really am. There's one more experimental thing they can try, but it has about a ten-percent shot at success. One in ten. It's ugly and painful and stands as good a chance of killing me as this thing does in the first place. Frankly, it sounds worse than everything I've had to do already all rolled into one." Patty looked at her. "And let's just say this awful treatment works. Do you know what I get? Two years, maybe three if I'm lucky. And then the odds of it coming back are still high. Even if it were free, I can't imagine taking it and it would cost a fortune. Does that sound worth it to you?"

"Living's not worth it?"

"Living? Spending most of my time stuck in a vinyl chair while they pour me so full of poison I spend the rest of the day vomiting is living? Swelling up or drying out or losing weight or whatever side effect of whatever drug shows up this week is living?" She thrust the pill keeper back into its spot in the basket. "I took care of your father. Every day. I know what that cost him. He was dependent. Humiliated. I don't want that." There it was, the it-has-been-decided voice Dinah knew so well.

Her mother was dying. Maybe because she had to, but mostly because she *chose* to. If an idea could attack a person, this is what it felt like. "But you asked me to come home." The idea of nursing Mom through a serious illness was bad enough. The idea of being here to walk her mom to the end was a thousand times worse. "I thought…" There wasn't even a way to finish that sentence. There weren't words for any of this. Dinah swiped at the tears she couldn't hold back. "I was sure you were exaggerating."

Her mother's voice lost all of its previous force. "You know, I wish I were," she said softly, reaching out to lay her thin hand across Dinah's arm. They'd hugged earlier, touched often, but there was always a tension in the touch. Now there was a quiet calm. They'd reached the worst point. It was horrible, but it was done. The tension was gone, but it left a frantic stillness in its wake. To Dinah, it felt as if she'd been swallowed by a fear so great she could only throw herself at God's mercy. Surely, she didn't have whatever it took to do what lay ahead. This was so beyond her. Even prayer felt impossible—as if the problem were so large and dark that words, even words of prayer, couldn't contain it. At the moment, Dinah didn't even know how she'd get out of bed tomorrow morning.

"You've had a long day, you look tired," her mother said, plucking a tissue from the box beside the medical basket. "We'll see Doctor Oliver tomorrow. He can fill you in on all the nasty details. Though, personally, I'd skip it."

Mom was so calm. So hopelessly calm. She's leaving already, Dinah thought, the stillness giving way to a cold, seeping panic. "No," Dinah said. Information was the only tool in her control right now. "I want all the nasty details."

Her mom stood up from the table. "Suit yourself," she said, collecting the still-full cups of tea. "He's handsome, Doctor Oliver. Single."

Dinah sank against the chair. "Mom…"

"I'm on the express train now, Bug, I can't afford to be subtle," she called over her shoulder as she shuffled toward the sink.

She was using that snarky tone Dinah always hated—and suddenly it was precious and fleeting. She pushed off the chair and practically ran to her mother, wrapping her arms around her from behind with such force the mugs clattered against the sink bottom. "Oh, Mom…" She was so much smaller than Dinah remembered. So much bonier. Defiant and sharp and frail all at the same time.

Aunt Sandy peeked sideways at her mixing bowl Tuesday morning. "Do y'all think it's supposed to be blue?"

"Blue?" Cameron glanced up from the spreadsheet where he was multiplying recipe ingredients.

Audrey Lupine, the town librarian, looked up from the

cookie sheet she was filling. "They are *supposed* to be blueberry muffins."

"Still," Aunt Sandy said, holding up a wooden spoon full of the surprisingly dark batter, "I'm wondering." The stuff looked like nothing Cameron would eat voluntarily. "They're supposed to be blueberry muffins. Not *blue* berry muffins. I'm sure I've eaten these at Dinah's and I'm equally sure they weren't blue. Well, not *this* blue."

It hadn't ever occurred to Cameron that Aunt Sandy couldn't bake. At all. He was beginning to wonder where Uncle George's generous midsection came from.

"It is a rather intense blue," Audrey offered.

It's almost black, Cameron thought.

"'Course I know Dinah does have a unique way of doin' things, but I did find it rather odd that her recipe said to blend those blueberries. It's not like we're making smoothies here."

Audrey put the last cookie on the sheet she was filling and walked over to Aunt Sandy's table. "Sandy, honey, where are your reading glasses?"

"Oh, I left them at home. I swear, I feel like I need six pairs of those things the way I keep losing 'em and leaving 'em places."

Audrey read the instruction sheet beside Aunt Sandy's bowl. Wincing, she caught Cameron's eye. "Well, it does say 'blend,' but it says 'blend in.' I think that's different."

"Well, now, I suppose you could say that's true. Kind of funny when you think about two little letters making all that difference, ain't it?"

Funny? Cameron pressed his fingers to his temples. He should go in search of rent-a-bakers. So far half the women's bell choir and a surprising majority of the Thursday Night Quilt Club had proved incompetent in the kitchen.

"Maybe retail's just more your thing," Cameron said, doubting the baked blue muffins would come out any more appetizing than the inky batter looked. "You can work the cash register better than anybody."

"Well, that's hardly a secret. This morning Shirley Bronson looked like the thing might spring up and bite her hand off."

That was true. Cameron had never worked a cash register, and even he knew to expect the cash drawer to automatically open at the end of ringing up a sale. Poor Shirley hadn't and that young woman let out an ear-piercing shriek when the drawer first slid out—and had nearly yelped every time after that. For the sake of all within earshot, Cameron reassigned her to cookie frosting after the first half hour. His worst day in real estate didn't hold a candle to his first day in retail baking.

It's only temporary, Cameron groaned to himself. Today and tomorrow. Somewhere in that horde of grandmothers had to be two or three master bakers. This was Kentucky, after all. Land of fried chicken and corn muffins. The baking country grandma stereotype had to come from somewhere—couldn't it be from Kentucky? Maybe he should just call the Grill and have owner Gina Deacon save the day—she could probably do this with one hand tied behind her back.

Still, there was something amazing about the sheer volume of people willing to help out. It wasn't like anything he'd ever seen before. Audrey Lupine was so happy to be spending her Tuesday—her day off—sliding frozen precut cookie dough squares onto baking sheets; she'd been humming show tunes for the last hour. And she'd burned only two of her eight batches.

If God laughed—and Cameron firmly believed He did—He was surely laughing now. *Just what spiritual gifts are You developing here, Lord? Patience? Self-control?* Oh no, this most certainly had to be a lesson in humility. Cameron Rollings, real estate magnate, the clever man who was now a full twenty days behind on his construction schedule, was currently inventorying chocolate chips. Cameron decided he would spend several hours next week pondering all the ways Howard Epson was going to make this up to him.

Chapter Eleven

Cameron didn't have to wait even one hour to give Howard his due.

Half an hour later, the entire "Coots" Bible Study arrived at the bakery in a group show of support. Whether it was for him or Dinah, Cameron didn't know. He didn't care. But it was just as he caught a whiff of yet another cookie batch burning that the idea came to him.

"Howard!" Cameron called, coming out from his managerial perch behind the counter. Even though his role was to organize and not to bake, he was dusted with flour and his jeans were smeared with…well, various baking ingredients. He'd switched to pen and paper an hour ago, fearing the migrating mess would spell the end of his laptop if he kept it down here any longer. "You're just in time."

"I am?"

Cameron walked up to Howard as if he'd been waiting all day to see him. "You remember telling me how much that horse of yours liked burned cookies?"

Howard gave him a puzzled look. "Not really."

Cameron clasped Howard's hand. Hard. "Sure you did.

You went on and on the other day about how you are always buying Dinah's burned batches off her. Personally, I think it's brilliant of you. Treats your horse nice and makes excellent use of local resources. It's practically eco-commerce—keeping food waste out of the landfill and all. I know I was impressed."

"Really." Howard was smarter than he looked. He saw what was going on. With the slightest grin and a look out of the corner of his eye that said "Touché, kid," Howard clamped a beefy hand on Cameron's shoulder. "I plum forgot we had that conversation until you mentioned it just now."

"I've been thinking about it all morning. Since I got up at the crack of dawn—before dawn, actually. Being up before the sun gives a man time to really think, don't you agree?" Cameron addressed that last question to the other four "old coots" who, having seen Howard's original "re-cruitment" of Cameron, were catching on and grinning themselves.

"Yep," agreed Vern. "Big fan of early rising myself." The quartet moved in around Howard, chiming in with "certain-lys" and "oh, yeses" and other agreements. Cameron was pretty sure Vern winked at him over Howard's shoulder. "I heard charcoal's good for horses. That's mighty smart of you, Howard."

"I like to think creatively," Howard said, looking around the room. "Keeps me on the cutting-edge, I think." He drew his words out just a bit, putting his hand in his pocket as if he'd already guessed this was going to cost him some-thing. "Always on the lookout, that's me."

Cameron couldn't hide his smile. "Wait right there. We've had a bit of a…learning curve this morning and I think today we have a bumper crop for you." Cameron offered up a chorus of thank-you prayers as he walked back to the kitchen for the garbage bag of burned cookies God had somehow prompted him to save. This was going to give a bigger jolt to his morning than two whole pots of coffee.

Howard gave a little whistle as Cameron plunked down the sizable bag. "I bet you're the kind of man who'd double his price if I told you I'll donate these as a pre-Cookiegram pledge," Cameron said. As Howard raised an eyebrow, Cameron pretended to go through his notebook of instructions from Dinah. "Dinah said you paid five dollars a pound. I'd say there's six pounds of burned cookies in this bag. That'd raise sixty dollars for the Community Fund in one transaction."

Vern began clapping almost immediately and within seconds the entire bakery—customers and volunteer bakers—broke out in applause.

"It's a mighty fine thing to donate to a good cause, isn't it?" Howard said, pulling his billfold from his pocket. "Bet you've been feeling that way all morning, helping out your new community in such an outstanding way." He peeled six ten-dollar bills off his billfold and laid them on the counter one at a time. "You're a regular tycoon here."

Aunt Sandy came up behind Cameron. "Oh no, Cam, honey, you just told me to man the cash register. Let me take care of that for you." She winked at Cameron and tapped his foot with hers behind the counter. The Bible Study "coots" were making unsuccessful attempts to hide their smiles, but Aunt Sandy wasn't even bothering to pretend she wasn't enjoying every second of this. "And let me just take this moment to publicly say," she said as she picked up the bills with all the drama Howard had used to lay them out, "how glad we all are to have such an enterprising young man as the newest member of our little town." She nodded toward the men behind Howard. "I think he'll go far, boys, don't you?"

"Amen!" said Pastor Dave. "He's a tycoon. Oh, wait, maybe he's not—maybe he's a ty*coot*." The room burst into laughter. "Now, what about the rest of us coots? You got anything back there that isn't burned?"

"Oh, I think Aunt Sandy and the ladies can set you up nicely," Cameron replied. "We haven't seen any smoke for at least half an hour."

It's Tuesday. They'll open my bakery today. Dinah hugged her knees to her chest in the post-midnight darkness of her mother's living room. Her living room, once. Her living room again?

She'd slept in fits and spurts last night. The doctor appointment had only applied clean, clinical terms to the horror of it all—her mother was right in that respect; the details didn't change anything. And yes, Doctor Oliver was handsome and charming in a way that surely impressed her mother, but how Patty had ever thought Dinah could see that man as anything other than the harbinger of doom, she'd never know. Even under the best of circumstances—which this was anything but—sane women just don't date their mother's oncologist. The fact that her mother had even considered fixing them up, and had even made broad, embarrassing hints to that effect during their appointment, still had Dinah shaking her head.

Oh, God, I can't do this. How can I get through this? This is miles beyond me. Don't do this to me. I know I have no right to say that, but You already know that's what I'm feeling. I'm begging You—don't do this to me. I'm not strong enough to take it.

A tear—the hundredth of the night—trailed down her cheek and she pulled out the packet of tissues she'd stuck in her back pocket. *I'll be keeping tissues in my pocket for a long time, won't I? Oh, Father, there's no way out of this, is there? I'm trapped, I'm trapped.*

I'm here, I'm here, she heard from down deep somewhere. *I'm here in the dark, I'm here in the fear. I will not leave you.*

"'Yea, though I walk through the shadow of the valley of death…'" she quoted to herself.

She got up and walked the house, wrestling with the challenge ahead of her. She loved the life she'd built in Kentucky. *How can You take that away from me now? How can You give me all that, all those people, and rip me away from them now?* And yet, the other choice facing her was just as compelling. *How can I leave her? I know we fight like cats and dogs, but how can I go now? This is…the* thought hit her like a physical sensation…*my last chance. I have to try.* What kind of human being would walk away from this? It was going to cost her everything she thought she loved. *Don't You know what You're asking me, Lord?*

She stumbled in the darkness on a basket filled with Christmas cards by her mother's couch. A plump, glowing baby Jesus looked out from the top card, reaching toward a maternal hand.

He did know. The realization nearly knocked the wind out of her, making her suck in a breath that was more of a sob. Of course God knew what it was like to lose something so dear you thought you wouldn't survive the loss. And really, she was being selfishly short-sighted—it wasn't like Middleburg was going to suddenly fall off the face of the earth. The weeks, months or years it took to walk Mom through this ordeal wouldn't stop her from picking up where she left off. If, at the end of all this, that's what she still wanted to do. She'd fought for years to bake—that drive and desire wouldn't go away with so important a detour.

Dinah picked up the card, one of the dozen classical Madonna and child Christmas card paintings. Who ever does family on their own terms? Mom had been candid about her early years of marriage in the many "you never really meet the perfect man" lectures she'd given Dinah over the years. Dinah knew things hadn't been wonderful between her mother and father when she was conceived. It hadn't been the right time to start a family. They'd been young, money was tight, her mom had just started a new job and both sets of parents were either too unhealthy or too far away to be of much help. And they'd just moved into town and hardly knew anyone.

They'd accepted those challenges. Now, perhaps, it was her turn. Dinah held the card to her chest. "Oh, Father," she whispered, sinking onto the couch with a terrible combination of peace and dread. "I've been an idiot. I have to do this. There's something really important in my doing this. But..."

She almost didn't dare give voice to the thought. But this was no time to hold back, no time to gloss things over. Life was about to get down to the nitty-gritty details. "What if we end up worse than ever? We couldn't stand each other on a good day. How are we going to handle the worst possible days?"

What if?

Perhaps, Dinah thought as she curled up on the couch, I'm about to find out just how big a God I really have. Maybe that old saying was true: there's no such thing as cheap grace.

* * *

"Morning, Bug," her mother said. She didn't look as if she'd had much more sleep than Dinah. "Don't like that bed upstairs?"

Dinah rolled over on the couch to find her mother sitting in the other chair, staring at her. Dinah was still in her jeans, the baby Jesus Christmas card crumpled against her shoulder where it had fallen as she slept. All the tumult was gone, replaced by a quiet resolve. The legendary Hopkins stubborn streak had a new focus and it felt this morning as if that focus had settled into her bones. She probably hadn't slept more than a couple of hours, but she was ready to face the day. Dinah stared at her mother, trying to think about how on earth they were going to survive the next few months.

The thought sliced through her, new and sharp. They weren't. Only she would. And while that seemed worse, it was in fact the thing that now held her here. She got to live. The least she could do was stick around, no matter what it cost her.

Dinah slid upright, feeling a collection of kinks two weeks of massages wouldn't undo. "I had trouble sleeping."

Her mom let her head fall against the side of the chair. She brushed aside the thick blue draperies to let in the first pale light of dawn. "I hardly sleep well ever anymore. It's partly all the little aches and pains, but I think I'm afraid of missing any more time."

She could say stuff like that so calmly. How does anyone ever make peace with something so terrible? What was that ad campaign, "Life Begins at Fifty"? It seemed like the worst joke in the universe at the moment. Dinah swung her feet to the floor. "You got any coffee in the house?" She'd gone out for coffee on their way to the doctor's office yesterday. "Do they even let you drink coffee?"

A tiny spark lit up the corner of Mom's eye. "I figure I can pretty much have anything I want now. I may just make a perfect pig of myself while I still have an appetite. Do they still make Funyuns?"

Again, how could she say that stuff?

Dinah's face must have registered the reaction, for Patty waved her hand dismissively as she hauled herself out of the chair with a groan. "I went and got some coffee Thursday. That horrible, strong stuff you used to choke down." She readjusted her thick pink bathrobe. "The acid in that will give you ulcers if it doesn't kill you first."

"Mom," Dinah groaned. "Could you make an effort here?" She padded toward the kitchen before her mother could come up with another macabre reference.

"And bacon. When's the last time you had a really good slab of bacon? All that sodium, all that fat. That turkey bacon tastes no better than the box it came in, if you ask me. Let's go out for a real breakfast today and eat something like that."

"Coffee first." Dinah combed her fingers roughly through her hair as she surveyed the kitchen for the coffeemaker. Her mother drank tea—maybe she hadn't even set it out yet. She turned to find her mother holding up a percolator coffeepot that looked like it hadn't seen the light of day since the Kennedy administration.

"Still works," her mother said, answering Dinah's raised eyebrow. "I had some friends over last week and we used it. 'Course I just fill the thing with instant and let it bubble away, but no one says a thing like they notice."

Dinah narrowed her eyes at her mother. Maybe not to

her face, but most people Dinah knew could tell the difference between instant coffee and brewed coffee. Especially when a tea drinker made it. She imagined the resulting beverage and winced.

"I do still have friends, you know. Here." With great drama, she handed Dinah a package of gourmet coffee from a local coffeehouse chain.

Yes! thought Dinah. Serious coffee and boy, do I need it. She had considered packing a half pound of her own brew from the bakery, thinking she'd need all the fortification she could get on this trip and not trusting her mom to stock up. With a hint of guilt at underestimating her mother in yet another way, Dinah undid the seal to inhale in the blessed aroma…

…and stared down at beans. Whole beans.

"Um…I'm guessing you don't own a coffee grinder, do you, Mom?"

Patty put the kettle on the stove. "What do you need one of those for when you buy it ground at the store?"

Dinah held out the bag to her mother. "Because you can also buy whole beans. To grind at home. Like you just did."

Patty blinked, reached into her robe pocket and fished out a pair of reading glasses, and then peered into the bag. "Well what fool would sell coffee you couldn't put right into your pot?"

Don't answer, Dinah told herself, just don't answer that.

"I guess you'll just have to settle for instant until I can take that back." Mom reached into the cabinet and pulled out an ancient-looking jar of store-brand instant coffee.

Instant coffee. *Oh, Lord, deliver me from instant coffee.* "You know, Mom, I'm thinking bacon sounds really good."

Chapter Twelve

Dinah had circled the room twice during her account of the trip to New Jersey. The woman was normally a bundle of high energy, but at the moment she was more like a bundle of nerves.

That bothered Cameron. He'd guessed what she'd come to say ten full minutes ago. Did she think him such a heartless capitalist that he wouldn't let her out of her lease to go home and take care of her dying mother? Is that the kind of image he really projected to the world? The kind of assumptions she made about businessmen?

"So…" Dinah said as she shifted her weight yet again, twirling one strand of hair around her right index finger—a nervous habit he'd come to recognize. "I need to do this. It's what I'm supposed to do. God showed me that so clearly while I was there. And I suppose under normal circumstances, I'd be able to give you more notice on the bakery and the apartment, but these aren't normal circumstances."

"Dinah…" He tried to stop the torrent of explanation. He'd expected this and had already decided what he was going to do. If he could only get a word in edgewise.

"I don't know what kind of penalties are in the lease and I'm not exactly swimming in extra cash to make this happen, but I can start looking for…"

"Dinah…" She obviously didn't realize she'd just paid this month's rent.

She hadn't even heard him. "…and it's not like you owe me anything—as a matter of fact I owe you so much, I mean you took over the bakery and you hardly even know me…" her voice was ramping up in volume and pitch as she went.

She was working herself into a frenzy over getting out of this lease. From a business standpoint, it should have been inconvenient and annoying. Emotional outbursts generally made him uncomfortable. He liked his relationships clean and elegant. And yet, her bluster of anguish produced an unexpected surge of sympathy within him. He knew—acutely— what it felt like to be dangling at the end of your rope. She was getting it from all sides and he had the power to make one part of this a little bit easier. Not that Aunt Sandy wouldn't have been as compassionate a landlord, but Cameron felt a deep, surprising satisfaction at being able to do this for Dinah.

"Dinah!" He grabbed her hand, trying to stop her frantic rambling. She whirled around at his touch and for a split-second he felt the inappropriate wish that the timing of all this had been vastly different. "I'm letting you out of the leases. No penalties. No problems."

Her eyes widened. "You are?"

Cameron still couldn't quite figure out how her voice could do that thing to him in just two words. "Do you think I'm such a cruel guy that I'd make this even harder for you? Like it's not hard enough already?"

"But it could be months before you get another tenant in here."

"I can handle it."

"Cameron Rollings, you're my hero."

It was like watching all the fear slip off the woman, all that dewy-eyed gratitude looking up at him like he was God's gift to Middleburg. It was hardly going to cost him anything to help her out.

She leaned in and kissed his cheek. Softly—and he was sure she never did anything softly—with something that was almost like a shiver when they touched. Cameron felt his eyes close as she lingered there a moment too long, the scent of her surrounding him.

She was vulnerable. Frightened and unsure. Battered by her current storm of feelings. She needed to leave; he needed to let her go. Help her go. Because, despite the hint of attraction he'd been denying since that basketball game, her leaving was the right thing to do.

He held his breath and stiffened his shoulders against her hug. She pulled back immediately, flushing and putting up her hands. It took him a second to realize she mistook his reaction and read his tension as offense rather than resistance. It wasn't a revulsion to her kiss—it was an attempt to stop himself from kissing her back.

Cameron's first impulse was to let her know he wasn't offended at all, but his logical side stopped him. It might be easier for everyone if he let her believe there was no interest. A few uncomfortable days, but that might help her to make a quicker, cleaner break of it.

"Oh, wow…um…I'm so sorry." Her hands came up to her face, mortified.

Cameron wiped his own hands down his face, both to hide his dumbstruck expression and to keep from saying anything that would give away what he was really feeling.

"That was…really stupid…I'm um…I'm gonna go." She fumbled out of his apartment and pulled the door shut behind her. He still hadn't moved. He listened to the slap of her flip-flops, heard her chastising herself in punctuated shouts that grew quieter as she made her way down the stairs.

As he heard the building door shut—slam actually— Cameron took stock of his sorry situation. He was jobless. He was now deeply in debt launching his new career as a developer—as an agent of change—in a community that hated change. Even if he won the name-change battle, there were still considerable challenges with the property soon to be formerly known as Lullaby Lane. He was behind on preparations for his exam in a few weeks because he'd somehow allowed himself to be wildly distracted running a bakery. He'd just been tempted to mix his business and personal lives—a peril he never would have considered in his former New York life.

The only thing that could make things worse would be to fall for the wrong woman at the worst possible time.

Dinah pretty much knew what kind of look she'd get from Janet when she told her the whole story of her last interaction with Cameron Rollings. And there it was—that half amused, half disappointed look perennially in-control people like Janet got when hearing about the antics of pe-rennially impulsive people like Dinah. "You kissed him," Janet said in the tone of voice one might use on teenagers out past their curfew.

"On the cheek. Chaste. Completely appropriate for such a huge favor," Dinah explained as they lingered in the lumber section of Janet's hardware store Friday after-noon. It was tucked in a back corner, far from the cash register, and as good a place as any to have so private a conversation.

Janet shot her a suspicious look while reshelving some long dowels. "Oh yes, I'd describe your current expression as 'chaste and appropriate' all right." Janet always did love to lay the sarcasm on thick. She turned and leaned in. "Why didn't you tell me you had a thing for him?"

"Because I don't. I mean really—Mr. Hypercapitalist? I heard they called him 'tycoot'—he probably thinks it's a compliment."

"You know what they say about opposites." Perhaps a woman in love was the wrong person to turn to for advice. Janet was knee-deep in her own case of "opposites attract" with Drew Downing. Dinah would have brought this problem to Emily, but she was caught up in her own romance as well with all those wedding preparations. Yep, Cupid seemed to be hanging around too much on Ballad Road these days and it was time she got herself well out of bowshot.

"There will be no romance with Cameron. I'm leaving. Fast. Before the end of the month, even. He knows that and I know that. And even if I were staying, this is hardly the time for me to even think about a relationship. Life is about as full as I can handle right now." She looked at Janet, suddenly aching for the strong friendships she'd made in her short time here. "I can't believe I'm actually leaving. Oh, God's gonna have to be really mighty here because I can't stand to leave Middleburg."

Janet pulled her into a hug. "One trauma at a time, okay?" She put both her hands on Dinah's shoulders and held her straight. "So you kissed him on the cheek."

"And I suppose you could say I lingered…a bit," Dinah

added, thinking complete honesty might be the best way to go.

"And evidently it was a bit beyond the standard grand-motherly peck variety of a kiss on the cheek. Let's take this one step at a time. Did he kiss you back?"

Dinah scowled. "He didn't. As a matter of fact, I think it made him pretty mad. I didn't exactly stick around to take a survey."

Dinah could practically see the gears in Janet's head turning, examining, collecting data. Janet was a champion problem solver—especially the emotional kind of problems—because she could distill things down to bare facts in a way Dinah never could. "So he's not interested. That's probably good. It would only make things worse."

"Of course it would."

"But he could still make things bad for you. He could go back on his word to let you out of the lease."

Dinah sat on the bottom rung of a ladder. "He wouldn't do that." She looked up at Janet. "Would he?"

"I don't know. He is Sandy's nephew and all, but I still think you ought to get his offer in writing. Actually, I think he has to anyway. It's a legal document, so if you change the details of the agreement, I think you have to do it in writing." She stopped shelving the lumber for a moment, one round piece held midair. "He's been extremely nice to you when you think about it. The oven, overseeing the volunteers for the bakery while you were gone, letting you out of your lease. You sure he doesn't…you know…expect any returns on his investment?"

"No!" Dinah couldn't believe she'd asked that.

"Hey, I'm just watching out for you. I have to think the

average New York executive landlord wouldn't be such a softy. God set it up perfectly, when you think about it."

He had, hadn't He? God had lined up all the details, clearing the path for her to go and do this huge thing that felt so beyond her capabilities. She had to keep holding on to that. God had provided all the logistical details—His provision wouldn't stop when it came to all the emotional strength she'd need. "Yeah," Dinah agreed, fighting the surge of that drowning, overwhelmed sensation that had threatened her nearly once an hour since deciding to move back home to New Jersey. "All except the part about leaving Middleburg."

"Home is wherever God plants you, maybe. It's not about the zip code."

That was a funny sentiment from someone who'd lived her entire life in Middleburg and now ran the store her father owned. "Middleburg is my home. New Jersey is my exile, my forty years in the wilderness."

"I'm sure wonderful people live in New Jersey. And besides, it's a seashore, not a desert, so it hardly counts as an exile."

"You haven't tasted my mother's coffee," Dinah muttered. "You have any boxes I can use to pack?"

Janet pointed to the storeroom. "I started saving the moment you called. Go talk to someone down at the bank and find out what you need to get in writing from Cameron. Once you've got it all down, the messy emotional stuff won't be a bother and you can just concentrate on getting yourself moved. By the way, what are you going to do about Emily's wedding cake? I'm assuming you're just off the Cookiegram thing altogether, right?"

Emily's wedding cake. That was the hardest of all. She'd

been up half the night the other evening, trying to think of a way to still make Emily's cake. There were ways to do it—to fly out a day or two early and do all the baking at the last minute or to hire out the layers and base frosting, swooping in to do the decorating the day before the wedding. But Emily didn't deserve compromises. The only true solution was to let someone else do the cake. They'd agreed when they talked about it yesterday, but it had made both her and Emily cry. She was giving up so much to go back east. She was feeling full-to-bursting with loss, which is why Cameron's act of kindness had touched her so. He'd given her what he could, for no other reason than it was a kind thing to do.

"I got another baker from Lexington to take the job." Dinah tried to say it calmly, but her pain clipped her words short.

"It'll work out," Janet said, sounding a bit choked up herself. "It has to. You've had enough pain already."

Chapter Thirteen

It was a sheet of paper. Of course, as a broker Cameron was well aware of the power a sheet of paper could hold, but he had mostly been on the sending end of that power, not the receiving end. Why should he be surprised that the crisis didn't stay, behind him, in his past?

The hysteria of running the bakery for two days had consumed his attention—running Taste and See had been a flexing of new muscles, a novel use for old organizational skills. Dinah's request to leave hadn't taken him by surprise, either; he'd been fully aware that once she'd worked up the nerve to visit her mother, she more than likely would go back and see her through this illness. Even before she'd returned, he'd decided to offer to let her out of the lease. It was the decent thing to do. Compared to all the other financial risks he was undertaking, going without a little rental income seemed a minor obstacle.

But this…this was a huge new obstacle. Or an old obstacle, depending on how you looked at it. When he'd first been fired, Cameron had contacted an employment attorney to sue Landemere Properties for how he'd lost his job. As he went through the initial process, discovering how lengthy and painful it would be, he'd opted out. He'd had moments of anger and betrayal, of course, but he thought he was done with that. He mastered that darkness— or so he thought—by distancing himself. Walking away without suing proved his nobility. Proved him to be the "bigger man" and let him get on with his life.

That same attorney had written now, reminding Cameron that the window of opportunity was drawing to a close. This was his last chance to change his mind and sue.

The possibility sent Cameron reeling. He could still sue. He had a strong civil lawsuit against his former employer, but it was getting close to his last chance to file.

It should have been a formality. A final double-check before closing the case. Instead, Cameron found himself knocked off his feet by an astoundingly dark hunger for revenge. As if the challenges of moving out here to Kentucky and the grief of all he'd left behind had been lying in wait, coiled to strike. He was overcome by the chilling urge to change course and get back at everybody before he lost his chance forever. To take his final shot at making them all pay.

Clutching the letter, Cameron seemed powerless to stop the catalog of offenses now building in his head. Even before things got really bad, Cameron realized he'd been nothing but a freak of ethics at that firm. All the looks. The good leads going to other brokers. When it came right down to it, he'd always felt like the only guy not out to make the largest buck possible in the shortest amount of time. But after he called the authorities, things got worse. Financing for his buyers started being turned down for idiotic reasons. Customers suddenly found themselves drowning in unreasonable requests or repeatedly "lost" documentation.

As he sat stunned at his kitchen table, Cameron knew what he ought to do. A man of faith should turn to prayer at a time like this, but Cameron felt as if that was impossible. These horrible, dark urges were not the impulses of a man of faith. These were not things to be shared with God. This felt more like Cain, avoiding God with Abel's blood still crying out from the ground at his feet.

He didn't even want to be in the room with himself. A fidgety itch hit him to go somewhere—*anywhere* but here. Hastily stuffing the letter into his pocket, Cameron pushed back his chair and left the apartment. *I'm not this man, am I?*

He paid so little attention to his movements that he nearly tripped down the stairs on his way outside. Outside seemed the best place to be, although he couldn't really say why. He toyed with the idea of going for a long run, just for the sensation of leaving his disturbing emotions behind, but ended up sitting on the park bench, instead.

He must have been there long enough to attract attention because he heard the distinctive slap of a pair of flip-flops behind him. "I haven't seen you move in the last fifteen minutes. I've got some paperwork to do about the apartment, so I brought you some coff…" The nervous but friendly tone in Dinah's voice faded as she came around to face him with two steaming cups of coffee. "Whoa, what happened to you?"

He'd wondered what he would feel when he saw her again. Perhaps this was a blessing, for he was so engulfed in feeling lousy that he hardly had space to even think about their last encounter.

She sat down next to him. Some small part of him

noticed she smelled as good as she did the other night. "Are you sick?"

Metaphorically speaking, that could be true. But as fond as Dinah was of her metaphors, Cameron lacked the energy for creative discourse. "I got a letter."

She set down her coffee on the bench and zipped up her jacket. Again, he thought of the absurdity of her bare toes and winter coat. But how was that any more absurd than the supposedly noble man who now found himself out for blood? "Letters," she sighed. "I know a bit about getting letters."

He didn't reply.

"So," she said after a moment, "this might be the part where you tell me what kind of letter has you so worked up." She looked at him as if an idea just dawned on her. "Oh, no. Did you just get a 'Dear Cameron' letter? Your chic urban girlfriend back in New York just dumped you, didn't she? Man, that's nasty."

Nasty. What an unsavory choice of words. For a moment he considered going with that story. It'd be so much easier. Instead, he slid the paper from his pocket and handed it to her.

She tucked one foot underneath her and skimmed through the letter. "I don't speak lawyer; I'm going to need a translation." Something in the text must have caught her eye though, because she got a more serious look on her face, put the paper down and turned to face him. "Wait a minute—are you being asked if you want to sue the guys who booted you out?"

"It's complicated."

"It's legal. That's a given."

"I don't really want to talk about it." Cameron felt like he wanted to go yell it from the top of a mountain. As if putting it into words would somehow force it to make sense.

"And you know how well that'll stop me. What's up?"

At that moment, he was insanely grateful for her annoying persistence. Dinah would drag it out of him and he needed it dragged out of him. Purged. Soon she'd be gone, so there was no harm in letting her in on his own private torment. He turned to her. "When I was still in New York, I started the process of suing my former employer. Not for financial scheming—they're already guilty of that—but a civil suit for how they treated me. For what they did to me professionally once I blew the whistle. And, I suppose, for the way they treated me before that, too. Me, and some other people." It sounded so simple when put that way. Like making a child apologize for calling someone a bad name. Nothing complicated like "punitive damages" or "class action settlements."

She looked back over the letter. "But you didn't?"

"I thought it would be best for everyone if I just walked away. The suit would be long and involved and probably very nasty. So I decided to pull the plug and just leave."

"And now?"

"I've got one last chance to change my mind and take them all down. I can still make them pay for what they did to me, if I act now. In a few weeks, that shot will be gone forever."

"I thought that's why you left, because you were all done. But you're not?"

"Not if I don't want to be." And that was the crux of it, wasn't it? Did he want to be done with it? Or did he want all the blood to be spilled?

"Were they that awful?"

"Yes," he said entirely too quickly. It was like all the anger came back in seconds. "No one had any illusions about my being able to stay on board after Frank was convicted, but I thought I'd at least be able to stay in New York."

"Frank. Was Frank your boss?"

"Yes and no. Frank was the head of the sister company, Landemere Finance. So he wasn't actually my boss, but he knew how to put the pressure on my boss. And my boss's boss." Frank was an orchestrator, a string-puller, and he'd given new life to the old phrase "You'll never work in this town again." There were days Cameron felt like he'd been marked by the Mafia, not one well-connected executive. The number of times he heard the sighed phrase "I'd like to help, but…" Even associates in his home state of Massachusetts had quietly considered him "too hot to touch." He could have found a position, played off his parents' connections for a mid-level management office somewhere safe, but the prospect felt sour to him. He didn't want that kind of personal or professional pity—not from associates or his parents. Their proud-but-worried attitudes suffocated him in the first days after his firing. As if they knew he'd done the right thing, were proud of him on some level, but would rather have had someone else's son take the noble fall. Cameron and his parents had a good relationship, but this was too much strain for everyone at the moment and Aunt Sandy's inquiry had felt like the perfect escape into a fresh start.

"So you'd be suing Frank now?" Dinah's question brought his thoughts back to the present.

"Sort of. He'd be personally named, but the company would be liable for allowing him to act the way he did. He was a snake, Frank. A real operator. I only stumbled on the evidence that he'd been in cahoots with a condo developer, skimming off money that new owners paid as 'assessments'—you know, payments for common costs like furnaces and roofs and such—and pocketing the funds instead of transferring them to the condo associations. I think I realized, on some level, that Frank was skimming off the top long before I went to anyone. And we all still did business with him. He hated me from the beginning, always treated me badly, but my boss always pushed the deals toward his finance office. I wasn't surprised customers started coming back with weird gaps in condo associations accounting or maintenance fees that we thought had already been covered. Frank and the condo developer were skimming off the assessments they'd inserted into the closing statements when people bought the properties, taking the money for themselves instead of sending it on to the condo associations to pay for things."

"But surely you must have known they'd slice you to ribbons once they found out you were on to them? Why on earth did you stay? If you knew they were so corrupt, why didn't you go find somewhere else to work?"

"I knew something wasn't right for years, that sneaky deals were being done, but dumb me thought I could do the whole 'light into the darkness' thing." He laughed weakly. "I had a high opinion of myself. You know, out to change the world, captain of the nobility team and so on. I told you, it's complicated."

Dinah sat back on the bench. "Yeah, I use that line, too." She tucked her other foot underneath her, so that she was sitting Indian-style on the bench beside him, as if it were a perfectly ordinary day. Go back inside, he thought. Bake things. Put some socks on before your feet freeze to death. Leave for New Jersey. Leave me alone.

Don't leave me alone.

"What he did was wrong. They *should* pay for it." After that declaration, she was silent for a long time, sipping her coffee. "Revenge looks so attractive, doesn't it?"

He started. Her voice was smooth and silky, as if she were one of those cartoon devils sitting on his left shoulder and whispering into his ear. "What?"

She turned and looked Cameron, spending a moment staring into his face. For a crazy second he felt like all those dark urges were visible to her, as if she had the ability to see the loathsome things he was feeling. Everyone in Middleburg thought he was such an upstanding guy, but she seemed to be able to tear off the sheep's clothing to see the wolf inside. "There's a big fat part of you that thinks you made a mistake back there in New York. That you should take 'em down, and make 'em pay. Isn't there?"

He shot off the bench. He didn't like her voice—that alto voice that slid into his thoughts—giving words to the things he was trying not to think.

"Hey, I'm not judging, I just wanted you to know I understand."

"Maybe," he said, not even looking at her.

He felt her pull on his jacket sleeve. "Sit back down." He resisted. "Cameron, sit down." It was the first time she'd said his name. It shone a clear beacon through the fog in his head. She yanked on him, hard. "Cameron Rollings, you big jerk, park it right now." He thought, at that moment, that she could easily be the little sister to eight burly big brothers, the way she could boss people around. He sat.

She waved the papers he didn't realize she was still holding. "You are not a monster. Wanting to get back at people for what was done to you? That's just human. Itching to take down some jerk because you've been given a golden opportunity to do it? That doesn't make you as bad as they are."

"Doesn't it?" he asked. He used to be better at keeping a lid on his emotions.

"The knee-jerk reaction isn't who you are. It's the choice you make with that emotion—*that's* who you are."

"You really like sticking your nose in other people's business."

"You really like changing the subject."

"No offense, but don't you think you've got enough on your plate without prying into my life?"

Now it was she who stood up. "You really don't get it, do you? No wonder Middleburg seems like a foreign country to you. We *are* in each other's lives out here. Because that's what caring is, what community looks like. You care about the guy next to you and he looks after you. It's a team sport, Mr. Basketball, that's what life here is like. I'm not prying, I'm trying to help. Trying, if that's okay with you, to give back a little of the whole lot you've already given me. If you want to sit here and refuse it, well, I suppose that's your choice." She sat back down again, finished with her rant. "Really, though, you'd be dumb to refuse it. People really like you here. You've made a great start of it. 'Tycoot' and everything."

She got that look on her face, the one as if another thought just struck her. "You," she said, pointing at him. "You're frightened of how much you like it here, aren't you? You just wanted to run off somewhere and hide, and we like you too much. We're in your face and it bothers you that you like it, doesn't it?"

"Do you analyze everyone like this? The town armchair therapist?"

She crossed her arms over her chest. "Again, you're avoiding the question."

"How did we get from my legal future to my psychological health?" Cameron remembered he'd prayed for distraction, but he was shooting for something a little more peaceful than Dinah Hopkins, Therapist-Baker.

"They're connected. That's just it, Cameron, it's all connected. *We're* all connected."

"Forgive me, but you sound a bit like a greeting card."

"See, that's what living in a humongous city can do to you. You get sucked into the cynical anonymity of the crowd. Here, you're a unique person, with distinct contributions. No cookie-cutter junior executives here, just God's amazing creation, each one of us."

He looked at her. "You just don't give up, do you?" He did, however, feel a shred better. He was going to miss her particular brand of lunacy. Her invasive energy. Her wicked left-handed layup shot.

"When do you have to decide what you'll do about the lawsuit?"

He looked over the letter, realizing he hadn't thought about that until she asked. When he'd first opened the letter, it felt like the whole decision had attacked him with urgency. "Next month." He didn't have to know what he was going to do about it now. He didn't even have to know what he was going to do about it tomorrow. He had time to work it out. Pray it out. Maybe even talk it out with someone like Pastor Dave. "I suppose I could figure out a lot by February."

"You could." She paused for a moment. "I'll be gone by then. Wow." It was like all the sparkle drained right out of her. She sighed heavily, looking out over the park. "Wow," she repeated more softly.

"You love it here, don't you?"

She nodded. "You will, too," she said after another shuddering sigh. "It's the most amazing place."

"Do you think you'll come back?" After a moment, he added, "That was a friendly question, not a landlord question, by the way."

It was a long time before she looked at him, her long lashes framing such sad eyes, and said, "I want to." She hugged her knees and tried to smile. "We don't always get what we want, though, do we?"

The wind picked up and Cameron realized they'd been out here a long while. He stood and extended a hand to help her up as well. "I have a feeling you'll be back someday."

"Oh," she practically breathed the word, "from your mouth to God's ears."

He chuckled. "I have an aunt who says that, too. Not Sandy, my other aunt. The calmer one."

"You get along well with your family?"

"Actually, yes. We'd bore you—all office types from New England who golf on the weekends and eat ham for lunch on Sundays after church."

"You mean Sunday *dinner*," she offered.

"Not in Massachusetts, we don't." He chuckled, thinking of his mother attempting a "y'all" in her broad Boston accent. He really couldn't have asked for a more stable, more solid upbringing. "Everybody back home does what they're supposed to, gets good grades, goes off to college to major in important things like finance and marketing and the occasional foreign language. Really, my exodus from New York was the most exciting thing to happen to my family in ages."

That brought a tiny laugh from her. "You couldn't say that about my family. I mean, we had all the trimmings, but the friction under the surface could shred you in seconds. My grandmother—my dad's mom—used to say 'from your mouth to God's ears' all the time," she continued as they headed back toward the bakery and his apartment next door. "She was more like Sandy, my grandmother. Mom is a bit more on the…unbubbly side."

Cameron couldn't quite picture the Hopkins family having an "unbubbly side." "Did you have something you said you needed from me?"

"Oh, just a letter stating you'll let me out of my lease. Janet said I ought to get it in writing just to dot all my I's, that sort of thing." She pulled a folded piece of paper out of her jacket pocket. Two corners were smashed and it had a coffee stain on one side.

Cameron laughed. Where he came from, legal documents didn't get folded in quarters and stuffed in pockets. They came in imposing envelopes delivered by serious couriers. He was starting to like the coffee-stained version better. "I've already drawn up a letter for you, Dinah. And Janet's right—it's always good to get those kinds of things in writing. Even here in Kentucky."

She stopped walking and looked up at him. "You're a good guy, Cameron Rollings. You know that?"

The woman did have a knack for asking just the wrong question at just the right time.

Chapter Fourteen

I didn't know I owned that much stuff, Dinah thought as she stared at the sea of boxes around her. Emily had offered to store some of her belongings up at their farm, kidding she'd hold it hostage until Dinah returned, but Dinah didn't have the strength to let herself believe she might get to come back. If she was going to leave, it had to be as if it were forever. She couldn't possibly know what the future held for her and her mother. Uncle Mike had called late last night to say Mom wasn't doing well, that he had offered to take her to the hospital, but she had asked to wait until morning. How long did they have? How bad would it get? Could she be strong if things got messy? What would she feel like when it was all…over?

Uncle Mike had called again very early this morning to say Mom had finally given in and they were heading over to the ER. He called half an hour later with an update. The doctors "didn't like the look of her" and were admitting her for observation. The storm outside this morning seemed to mirror the one in Dinah's heart.

"This isn't the first time this has happened," Uncle Mike had said. "I think we'll all be glad when you get here."

And she was leaving—really—soon. Someday soon she'd finish her last batch of sticky buns. Even though thunder and lightning slashed their way across the valley, Dinah had relished the numbered last mornings in the sanctuary—and that really was the right word for it—of her bakery at dawn. Some part of her still couldn't believe she was closing her bakery. Someday, all too soon, all her friends would help her load the rental van. Then she'd get up early one morning, only it wouldn't be to turn on the ovens—it would be to turn onto the highway.

The phone rang just as the last of the thunder rolled over the mountains. "Dinah," came Uncle Mike's tense voice, "how quickly can you get on a plane?"

Cameron was shaving when the doorbell rang. Followed by an insistent knock. Too nice to be Dinah, but he wasn't sure who else would be banging on his door at eight in the morning. When he opened it, Janet Bishop stood on the other side, an unmistakable look of alarm on her face. "Got a minute?" she asked.

"Sure. Everything okay?" Cameron toweled the last of the shaving cream off his face as she walked a few steps into his apartment.

"It's Dinah. Her mom took a turn for the worse overnight—some kind of infection—and things got bad. She went downhill so fast. We were trying to get Dinah out of here on a plane, but the weather loused everything up."

Cameron thought he'd heard more commotion than usual down in the bakery. Dinah didn't need this now.

"We were just getting ready to leave for Louisville,

thinking we could get her on a stand-by ticket, when…
when the phone rang." She paused and Cameron realized
things were far worse than Janet's calm let on.

"What is it, Janet?"

"Dinah's mom…" Janet's eyes welled up. "Well, she
died…about an hour ago."

"Oh no."

"Dinah was able to talk to her one last time—they held
the phone up to her ear and Dinah got to tell her she loved
her, but…" Janet looked like she'd been crying, but she also
had that no-nonsense, take-charge demeanor he'd seen over
his weeks in Middleburg. "Emily's been with her since the
first call. I got here around seven. We're sort of figuring out
what to do from here. I thought you'd want to know."

"How can I help?" Cameron shook his head, the full
brunt of the news coming to him. *Dead.* "Dinah must be
devastated."

"She's pretty messed up right now, but we're calling in
the cavalry. I thought maybe you could keep the apartment
for her for another month, you know, until she figures out
what to do. That way she can just fly out now to take care
of the funeral and worry about the long-term stuff when
she's a little less stunned."

"Of course, yes. I hadn't even started looking for a new
tenant. Tell her I'll hold both the bakery and the apartment
for another month until she has a chance to figure things out."
He looked at Janet. "Do you think she'll decide to stay?"

Janet sighed. "I don't think she should try to decide right
now. She just needs her friends around her, taking care of the
details on this end so she can do what she needs to do on hers.
I just thought it might be nice to have that detail wrapped up
right away so she doesn't need to worry about it."

"Tell her not to give it a second thought."

Janet offered a small smile. "Why don't you go tell her yourself in about an hour? She could probably use all the friendly faces she can get today."

"Count on it," Cameron replied. "You're a good friend to her."

"She's a good friend to me. I'll miss her something fierce when she goes." She choked on the last two words, sniffing back the tears that threatened to return.

Cameron put out a hand. People cared so much about each other here. If anyone's world had to fall apart, Middleburg was a good place for it to happen, amongst such strong friends. "Maybe we can change that to 'if she goes'—but not today. Today let's just get her through the fire, and we'll leave the fate of her sticky buns to God for the moment."

Dinah stood amid a maze of boxes, red-eyed and frail-looking. Janet was downstairs doing something in the bakery and Emily was making phone calls in the kitchen. It was the first time Cameron had ever thought of her as frail. Even when she was dealing with the "come home" command from her mother that afternoon in her kitchen, she'd never been frail. Even the tears she shed that night held a strength behind the sadness. Now her shoulders sagged and she looked pale and wan. She had the fight beaten out of her. "Um, hi," she said unsteadily as he came into the room.

"Dinah, I'm so sorry." He walked straight to her—or as straight as he could, navigating through the boxes—and gave her a quick, heartfelt hug. "I'm just so sorry," he said, holding on to her arm for a moment.

She pulled her arm from his grasp with a shaky sigh and wiped her eyes. "You know that vocabulary you wished you could have used?" Sniffing, she dug a tissue out of her pocket. "That day back in New York when they canned you?"

While he wished she'd put it a little less bluntly, he turned up one corner of his mouth and said, "Yes, I remember."

"I think I know how you felt. It's all just so…rotten. So wrong and horrible and…when I'm not crying I just want to scream and hit things."

That sounded just a bit more like the Dinah Hopkins he knew. "I'd say you're entitled."

She began to wander among the boxes. "She had more time coming to her, you know? I know she may not have had much, but she needed more than this. She deserved more than this. I was moving out there. We deserved more time than we got."

He started to say something, then wondered if she didn't just need to talk it out. "It's stopped raining. Do you need to get some air for a minute, Dinah? My dad always told me sometimes the best thing to do in a crisis is to walk it out. I've got to take something to the mailbox. Want to walk with me?"

"You know, I think that might be a good idea," Emily said as she came in from the kitchen. She had a long list on one of those yellow note pads, the top third of which had been crossed off. The cavalry had indeed been called in. "You should get out of all this chaos and take a couple of minutes to catch your breath. It'll be a long day no matter what you do."

"Have you eaten any breakfast?" Cameron asked, picking up Dinah's jacket from where it lay on a stack of boxes near the door.

"Janet made me some eggs and toast. I think I ate half of it."

"So we'll just walk. We'll cut through the park so you don't have to talk to anyone if you don't want to. There's a mailbox down by March Avenue. And we'll come right back if that's what you want." He wanted to scoop her up and tell her it would all be okay, but just like his last day at the office, everybody knew there was no "okay" to be had right now. She was in the fishbowl of catastrophe, with everybody staring in. Wanting to help, but staring in just the same.

"Okay," she said in a monotone. "Sounds good."

He led her down the stairs and against his better judgment, he took her hand in his as they headed toward the park across the street. "Look up at the sky," he said. "Look up at the storm clearing off and remember the world is bigger than the dark place you are in today."

She made a poor attempt at a laugh. "That's awfully poetic for you."

He squeezed her hand. "It was something my dad said to me the day I was *canned*." He used her verb. "Although I don't think walking down Sixth Avenue in Manhattan is quite the same as enjoying this."

"I couldn't see God without all this nature," Dinah offered, her voice sounding close to normal for the first time that morning. "I think it's one of the reasons I like it here so much." She swallowed so hard he could hear it. "I like it here *so much*."

Cameron tightened his hand around hers in reply. They walked a minute or so in companionable silence, making their way through the patchwork of pine trees and slushy puddles that looked more beautiful than any winter Cameron had slogged through in New York. He waited a long time before he dared to say, "Maybe you can come back." He wanted her to know she had someplace to go when all this trauma was over. "I mean, it's impossible to say what will happen, but just know I won't do anything with the bakery and your apartment until you've had a chance to make up your mind. Now's not the time to worry about that, though. You've got enough on your plate."

Dinah took another deep breath, shrugging her shoulders and picking her way around a puddle the way she always had to in those insufferable flip-flops. "I don't know."

He squeezed her hand again. "That's what I'm saying. You don't have to know. I've got your back. Hey, I'll even water your houseplants—seeing as I don't have any yet."

Something close to a laugh trickled out of her. "Janet's got that covered. And she finally found me a flight out of Lexington. One-thirty this afternoon. She offered to get me a round-trip ticket—something called an 'open-end return,' but I'm flying one-way." She shook her head slightly, her red hair tumbling around her face as she continued to look down.

At first, he'd thought her hair color an affectation— rather like all of Sandy's hair-sprayed updos. Now, he couldn't imagine her in any other color or with anything less than that long, wavy storm of curls framing her face.

"I didn't even know there was such a thing as an open-end return," she continued, pulling out of his grasp to run her hands over the bronze statue that stood at one end of the park. It was of a foal and a mare, reflecting the town's deep connection with the thoroughbred world. "I don't know lots of things anymore." She grazed her hands over the knobby legs of the baby horse then turned to look at him for the first time since they'd stepped outside, pain in her eyes. "I don't know where my faith is right now. I feel everything and I feel nothing. I know the belief is still in there somewhere, but I can't feel it." The corners of her eyes welled up. "How can I hang on to it if I can't feel it?"

Cameron wished he were a champion of faith, a spectacular man of God who could produce the perfect answer. He yearned for a powerful faith, so that he could somehow lend it to her, shore her up for the challenge ahead. But his own faith was feeling as wobbly as the newborn legs of the statue. He had nothing to give her. Nothing except his own history of having the rug pulled out from under him. And as traumatic as his loss had been, tanking a career paled against the sorrow of losing a parent so suddenly. He'd had a golden life compared to hers.

"I think you're in shock," he offered. "Spiritually, emotionally and probably even physically. Nothing will be clear today. Today's the day when you count on your friends to do the thinking for you. The only thing you can do today is get through it. I don't think your faith has fled the scene. Think about all the people praying for you. Emily's called Aunt Sandy by now for sure and you know how Sandy Burnside can call the faithful into action. You've got friends and faith and you're the toughest redhead I know. You'll come out okay no matter what."

"I *do* have friends," she said as they reached the mailbox. She took another deep breath, this one less shaky than the last and held out her hand toward him. "I got me a few new ones, too."

He couldn't help but smile. "Who'd have thunk it?"

"Certainly not me when you first barged into my kitchen. That seems like years ago, now."

"And here I thought I'd be bored out in the middle of nowhere."

"Oh, we're lots of things here in Middleburg, but boring is never one of them. Did I ever tell you Emily tied a gift bag of soap from her shop to this mailbox once? She was helping Peter Epson woo Megan Walters. Megan was a mail carrier, and Peter and Emily came up with the idea to fix a bag of goodies and leave it waiting for her right here on her birthday, about a year ago. It worked. They're engaged now, Peter and Megan. Imagine."

"No kidding?" It sounded crazy, but based on his short residency in Middleburg, it was easy to believe.

"Yeah, we all got a kick out of it." She pulled open the mailbox slot for Cameron as he fished the envelopes out of his coat pocket. "I was gonna spend so many afternoons telling Mom about all the kooky stuff that happens here. You know, take her mind off…the pain…and all." Dinah lost her battle with the tears and Cameron lost his battle with his resistance to hold her. He pulled her into his arms. She melted there and Cameron sent up a silent prayer of thanksgiving for the privilege of holding her while she cried. And it felt like a privilege, a service. He realized, with a sudden solidness, that if one of the only reasons God had landed him in this odd little town was to hold Dinah Hopkins at this moment, then that was okay with him. He held her as tightly as he knew how and just whispered "It'll be okay" every once in a while until she cried it out. You could never do this in Manhattan, he thought, but you can do it here.

"I'm sorry," she said finally, pulling back to point at the dark patch her tears had left on his leather jacket. "I've left a spot."

You've left much more than that, he thought as he looked

at her. She'd left something inside of him, something he'd be so sorry to lose if she never came back. "I'll be fine," he lied.

"I should get back. Pack and all." Still, she didn't move from his embrace.

He shouldn't. It was the wrong time and a terrible place, but it didn't seem to matter. Gently, Cameron leaned in and kissed her on the forehead. He felt his eyes close and his heart tumble in his chest, felt the curls of her hair tickle at his chin, felt a little tremble in her as he lingered there.

"If you don't come back…" he started to say and then realized he couldn't finish the sentence. *I don't want to regret never having kissed you? I'll not know why I'm here? I'll miss you?* None of those things was the slightest bit appropriate for the situation. He shouldn't even have ventured to kiss her forehead in the first place. But oh my, he couldn't remember when a tender gesture stunned him as much as this one did.

She smiled softly, weakly, and Cameron thought the word "deflated" had never fit a human being more. It was like he was looking at an echo of Dinah, not the vibrant woman who had sneaked into his thoughts. "I suppose we'll just have to leave that up to God," she said. "Just…just keep praying for me, okay? Keep them all praying."

She turned back toward the bakery and Cameron thought how wrong he had been to kiss her when she was so extraordinarily vulnerable. *Oh, Lord,* he moaned in his heart as he watched her take a few steps away from him, *don't let me mess this up.*

She turned and looked over her shoulder. "Well," she held out a hand in his direction, "are you coming?"

He caught up with her, feeling a piece of his heart leave him. It would follow her, he was sure, all the way to New Jersey, never to return.

Chapter Fifteen

Two days later, Uncle Mike stood in the kitchen of Dinah's mother's house—or was it Dinah's house now?—and surveyed the overflowing counters. "Funerals sure do make people hungry, don't they? I thought your cousin Frederick was going to confiscate every shrimp in the house the way he was going at the buffet table."

Dinah couldn't laugh. They'd just buried her mother. Who cared about how many shrimps cousin Frederick ate? Still, it was hard to believe that person in the casket was Patty Hopkins. Everything about her mother's face seemed wrong and unfamiliar, her clothes perfect but somehow all wrong, her hands bearing the correct rings but shaped all wrong. Only the photographs—the myriad of portraits and snapshots and Christmas card photos they'd mounted around the room at the funeral home—seemed to show the real Mom.

Uncle Mike's hand slipped onto her shoulder. "You okay?"

"No."

He leaned wearily against the counter. "That's the right answer, Dinah. Don't go trying to make it all okay just yet. It was a terrible shock to all of us—most people didn't even know she was as sick as she was. Respect your grief and give it time."

Give it time? Respect it? Did she have a choice? It held her hostage, wrapped itself around her so that even the smallest tasks felt monumental. Finding containers for the leftover food felt like a challenge beyond her strength. "Yeah," was all she managed, forcing herself to start opening cabinets and looking for things like aluminum foil. She'd grown up in this house, but she'd been gone so long she couldn't remember where things were in the kitchen. The choke hold of grief threatened to overtake her again.

Uncle Mike put his hand over hers where it was tugging on a drawer. "She was so glad to have you coming back home. It was all she talked about. I know you two had trouble finding a way to get along, but it meant the world to her that you were going to come back. Maybe that's why she could leave. The hospital chaplain told me that dying people often hold on for the one thing they really need, then they seem to be able to let go. She held on until you two reconnected and then, I guess, Patty could let go."

Dinah looked up at her uncle, too overcome to make any reply.

"It's better for me to think of it like that. That way, it feels like Patty got what she wanted, instead of being robbed of her last days. And you know your mom." He choked up a bit and held her hand tight. "She always got what she wanted." They fell into each other's arms and Dinah heard her uncle weep for his baby sister for the first time since they'd begun the exhausting funeral preparations. "You can come stay with us tonight," he said when he finally straightened. "Shannon thinks you should." Aunt

Shannon was always certain she knew what other people needed and often rather insistent about giving it to them.

"Thanks, but I want to stay here." Dinah needed silence, needed to be surrounded by her mother's things. How many times in the past two days had she stood in front of her mother's closet, just running her hands over all the clothes? Outfits she long remembered, others she neither recognized nor could picture her mother wearing. How had they grown so distant? And now, that gap loomed uncrossable, that estrangement fixed forever this side of heaven. Dinah regretted so much it took her breath away. She mourned both her mother and the goodbye they didn't really have. It was a double-grief that stole the hopeful person she used to be and left a numb shell in its place.

"You're sure?" Mike blew his nose on a handkerchief from his pocket before he reached for his coat. "You'll be okay?"

"No," she said, remembering his earlier advice, "but I'll be here in the morning."

He gave Dinah an understanding smile. "Shannon and I will come by at ten and take you to breakfast. Might as well tackle all that paperwork on a full stomach."

Howard Epson opened his barn doors and ushered Cameron inside. "I was going to ask you an important question, but I think I'd better ask you what's wrong first. You look miserable. Started looking for a new renter yet? I told Peter to talk to you about running an ad in the paper. You could even move in there yourself, now. Have you thought of that?"

"No, I'll put in an ad when it's time, but I told Dinah I'd hold both of the spaces for her for a month or so, until she gets her plans worked out."

Howard took a bucket off the wall and began scooping some kind of feed into it. "That's mighty nice of you. I reckon that helps smooth things out a bit." He handed the bucket to Cameron to hold as he added two cubes of something that looked like hay and a trio of different powders.

"It seemed like the least I could do."

"It's more than that. You've done a lot for her and for the town in the short time you've been here. I like that about you. Reminds me of myself when I was your age. Not afraid to jump right in and get involved."

Cameron thought it was more like Howard had dragged him in far earlier than he was ready to get involved, but he kept that to himself.

"You got those building permits all lined up for that house of yours?"

"I'm behind, but we're getting there. First set of forty-degree days and we should be able to pour the foundation."

"Good. So, then, what's really getting under your skin, Rollings?"

What and who, if you want to get right at it. Then again, Cameron had actually planned to talk over his legal dilemma with Howard. He'd taken a tremendous liking to the puffed-up old man, as if his lack of Middleburg history had enabled him to see a side of Howard Epson no one else could. Cameron suspected Howard was willing to be a target, willing to be the guy everyone complained about, if it got things done in town. Willing to play "bad cop," as it were, because someone had to make the hard or unpopular choices a struggling town needed to make. Sure, he had faults—loads of them, actually—but Cameron was feeling pretty faulty himself these days and while he couldn't explain his kinship with Howard, he couldn't resist it, either.

"Howard, have you ever found out something about yourself that you really didn't like?" Cameron hadn't meant to start out quite so bluntly, but there was something about the quiet of the horse barn, the companionship of walking with this older man through the slatted sunlight and warm hues. He found himself desperate to talk about it with someone. "I mean, thought you did something for a noble reason, only to discover you really only did it to serve yourself?" He added after a second, "Maybe even for an uglier reason than that?"

Cameron was glad Howard didn't reply right away, but gave his question considerable thought as they walked toward the stalls at the far end of the barn. "I have," he said eventually, "and I remember it making me pretty miserable. Perhaps not too far from the way you look now, son. A man meets himself in those dark corners, and I reckon everyone's got them, but only the wisest of us are ready to own up to it." They'd reached the stall and Howard said hello to his horse in warm, grandfatherish tones as he gave her the feed. Once the bucket was dumped out, he stroked the mare fondly for a moment or two, then turned his attention to Cameron. "I find it's much easier to solve problems if you know what they are. How's about you come out with whatever it is that's eating you?" Howard pushed open a door that led out to the pastures. "Don't worry, I won't think less of you to find out you're human just like the rest of us, even if you do come from that big city out east."

"I don't know how much Aunt Sandy's told you about my abrupt departure from New York."

"Enough," Howard said, stuffing his hands in his pockets. "'Whistle-blower loses job' isn't so new a story.

Sounds like you lived it on a slightly larger scale, though. Takes bravery on any scale, if you ask me."

"I thought I was being brave. I was sure I was doing it for the right reasons. For justice and to keep people from being hurt. All the classic stuff—righting a wrong, standing up for the truth and so on. And all through the state attorney's proceedings, I believed it." Cameron reached down and picked a twig up off the brown earth, turning it over in his hands. "I admit, I liked the way people thought of me after I'd done it. I became the hero instead of the moralizing Puritan everyone stared at. I don't think they liked me, but I felt like they respected me."

"It's no sin to want respect. Men are hardwired to want that. To know we occupy a place in the world." The way Howard said it, it sounded like he was quoting one of his own speeches. Affected, but heartfelt just the same.

"After the criminal trial, I started the process of personally suing Landemere. Then I decided against it, thinking it was a better choice to just walk away. I've been given a final chance to change my mind, though, and go through with it."

"And will you?"

"My plan was to leave it behind me. No revenge, no after-battle, just a clean getaway. But now…"

Howard sat down on a large log that ran beside the path they had been walking. "But now, with the last chance in front of you, you're surprised at how much you'd like to take it."

Cameron stood still, startled by Howard's exact assessment. "Burning with it. I didn't think I was that kind of man. I shouldn't be that kind of man. And now as I look back at everything I did at Landemere Properties, I realize I blew the whistle for the wrong reasons. I blew it to hurt Frank. Not even because Frank was doing wrong, but because he treated me so badly. I just wanted to take him down. And now I still do. I hate that I could do that and fool myself that I was being some sort of hero." Cameron couldn't decide how it felt to say those words out loud. He was both freed and condemned by the admission, which mostly just left him miserable and confused. He sunk onto the log next to Howard, not daring to look the man in the eye.

Howard stretched out his legs in front of him. "So you did the right thing for the wrong reasons."

"All the wrong reasons. All the worst reasons."

"Hard to live with, ain't it? To know you're capable of the same evil they are."

Cameron couldn't help but look at Howard now. "That's just it—it makes me just like Frank. He was such a creep and now who's to say I'm not just like him?"

"Well, I think you've hit on it—'Who's to say?' I think we are who we decide we are. We're all capable of horrors, Cameron. Little ones and big ones. It's the man who forgets that who shows himself to be foolish. The moment I forget I'm a pompous old windbag, I'll just be a fool instead of a man willing to be pompous for a good cause. Maybe you just have to be mean for a good cause."

"That makes no sense."

"Well, now," Howard chuckled, "you're just young enough to still expect the world to make sense. Life looks black and white when you're young. Clear-cut and all. Once you put on a few years and a few pounds, you discover there's more fuzzy gray than you ever signed up for. The question becomes, what are you going to do with all that fuzzy gray?"

"Meaning am I going to sue or not?"

"Well, that's part of it. Only you can decide if your

reasons for calling the cops on that man in the first place have any bearing on whether or not you want to go forward with a lawsuit. Your motives—however pure or impure—don't change the wrong he was doing. Never confuse the facts with your interpretation of them—that's what I always tell Peter."

That was good advice for a newspaper reporter. It was rather obtuse advice for a man facing the moral dilemma Cameron was facing. "Are you saying I should just look at the facts before me and not get so caught up in who I think they make me?"

Howard stood up. "Actually, I'm saying I think you should make cookies."

Cameron looked at him. With his mouth open, probably. The man went from being wise to making no sense at all. "Huh?"

"You're just now figuring out who you are outside of that job. Outside of New York. So be who you are here, in Middleburg. And that, for better or worse, is the guy who can get cookies made." Howard planted a beefy hand on Cameron's shoulder, like he always did before he was about to make one of his unrefusable suggestions. "And we still need cookies made. The Cookiegram fund-raiser is two weeks away and we just lost our baker. But what we do have is a bakery, volunteers and a young man who's proven he can manage them pretty good. And that young man just happens to have a little time on his hands and a lot of thinking to do." He gave Cameron's shoulder a squeeze and started back toward his barn. "That's what I had you come up here to talk about. Makes more sense than ever to me now."

Cookies did not solve moral dilemmas. Cameron was

facing slightly larger problems than the logistical threat to Middleburg's inaugural Cookiegram fund-raiser. Perhaps his affection for Howard had been misplaced. Or dead wrong.

"You've got to be kidding."

"No, I think this is just the ticket. You need something simple to do with undiluted goodness attached to it. Do you have to give your response to this lawsuit thing right away?"

Lying, saying he had to fly to New York to consider his options within the next twenty-four hours, suddenly seemed like a good reply. Instead, he said, "Um, not really."

"It's settled, then. I'll have Sandy call you this afternoon. I've asked her to double up on the volunteers she got you last time."

He asked Aunt Sandy? *Before* he asked him? Suddenly his own arrogance seemed minor in comparison to the assumptions Howard made. And as for Aunt Sandy, she had probably egged him on—thought it was a stellar idea. This was Dinah's blessed "community" gone horribly wrong.

Dinah was making piles out of the memorial gifts and condolence cards, trying to sort them in some kind of order, when her cell phone rang. Cameron's number flashed on the screen, and she gave a small smile as she flipped open her phone. "Hello?"

"Hey, how are you?"

She remembered Uncle Mike's admonition. "I'm here."

"How was the funeral?"

Dinah got up from the kitchen table where she had been working and walked onto the sun porch. It was a gray winter day, but she still preferred the room to any other in the house.

"It was nice, actually. Lots of people came, the music was beautiful, and when the pastor invited everyone to come up and tell 'Patty stories,' it became a real celebration of all the things Mom did in her life. I actually heard stories I'd never heard before. That felt really nice, you know? As if it's not all over, just one part of it is."

"I'm glad. I always thought funerals should be sad celebrations but still celebrations. They don't always seem to work out that way, but I was praying it would for you."

He'd been praying for her. That made something hum in her chest.

"Everyone's been praying for you," he added, as if he'd somehow sensed her reaction over the airwaves and didn't want to get too personal. "Check the mirror. You might just be glowing, there's so much prayer headed in your direction."

"I thought I felt something funny run down my spine a minute ago." It struck Dinah that she'd just made her first joke since her mother died. It was a good feeling. "And here I thought it was just exhaustion."

"Those things are exhausting, aren't they? I'm guessing you have so many tasks ahead of you it's hard to know where to start."

"I've come up with a strategy of sorts in the two days since the funeral. Every time I think of something that needs doing, I put it down on this big yellow pad. Then I take an index card and pick five things to do off the yellow pad and put the pad out of sight. I just work off the index card until I'm ready for another one. The first day I tried and I got through two cards. Yesterday I didn't get anything done. I think it's gonna be like that for a while."

"That sounds really smart. Hey, maybe you should make one more index card with things other people could do to help you. That way when you get all those 'let me know if I can help' calls, you'll be ready."

Dinah sunk down into the chair and put her feet on the coffee table. She stared up at the collection of hanging plants in the sunroom. She should try to remember to water those. "That's a pretty smart idea yourself. Want to come over and water Mom's plants for me?"

"I have a black thumb. Plus, that's a pretty long trip. But there is one thing I can do. Do you have access to e-mail?"

"Mom's got a computer, yes."

"If you give me your e-mail address, I'll refer you to two local real estate brokers I've found. You'll need someone to help you with an appraisal of the house, whether you decide to stay or not." There was just the slightest hesitation before he said "or not." She didn't know what to make of that. She still didn't know what to make of the astoundingly gentle kiss he'd placed on her forehead the day she left. How many times over the past four days had she touched her forehead, unable to stop thinking about how tender the kiss had been. How potentially dangerous it was. If she went back to Kentucky, it would be her head making the decision, not some tingly spot on her forehead. She owned a house now. The only family she had left was here. These things had to be taken into consideration.

"That's nice of you." She gave him the address and told him to go ahead and send it, being careful to point out she didn't know what would happen from here or when she'd be able to make any kind of decision.

"It's been only a few days. Stick that on your yellow pad and you'll get to it when you're ready. Are you baking?"

"Am I what?"

"Baking. I just thought maybe you'd bake out of—I don't know, comfort, I suppose."

She hadn't even thought about baking. Now she thought

about how much less empty the house would feel with something in the oven. "Well, you're just full of good ideas, Mr. Rollings. No, I haven't baked, but it's an idea." She pulled the index card out of her pocket and wrote "bake" above the other five items. Suddenly it seemed like she couldn't turn the oven on fast enough. "A really good idea."

"I just can't picture you not baking, that's all. It'd be like cutting off a hand or something. It's what you do."

Dinah let herself smile. "When did you get all insightful?"

"Since I had to start baking."

Chapter Sixteen

Dinah bolted upright. "Since you started *what?* Did you just say 'baking'?"

"Well, that's sort of the other reason why I called. Howard's decided the Cookiegram thing needs to go on. So he put me in charge of staffing volunteers to use the bakery to make all the cookies. Sort of an extended tour of duty from last time."

Dinah actually laughed out loud. "Oh, that sounds like Howard all right. You're not really going to do it, are you? You've got your exam and all."

"I don't think I have a choice. I've been ambushed, exam or no exam. Sandy helped him."

"Oh, you really are outnumbered." She laughed again and some of the knots in her chest came undone, like an unlaced corset letting her breathe again.

"I was hoping you could give me a few pointers on running this kitchen for more than a pair of days. You know, a *Cookies for Dummies* kind of thing. I'm thinking if we stick to two or three common recipes it'll be less crazy than if everyone does their own thing."

Dinah cringed. "Can't Sandy do this?"

There was an odd pause on the other end of the phone. "It's become sort of a pride thing now. I refuse to admit I can't do it. Take that secret to your grave, okay? Oops, sorry. That probably wasn't the most sensitive thing to say."

Dinah was amazed how many people had edited death out of their language in the past five days. It was funny, having now looked death in the face through both her parents, it didn't loom as a horrible specter for her. She'd survived it. Twice. "It's okay. I'm too tired to take offense at anything tiny like that."

"Still. But really, how are you feeling about everything? How are you holding up?" She felt like he stopped just short of saying "I'm worried about you."

"I'll get through it. I just don't know how or when."

"You have a really strong faith, Dinah. That's *how*. The *when* doesn't make that much difference."

"Said the landlord." She meant it jokingly. Sort of.

"Don't do that. I don't want you to think like that." His voice got rather quiet and she imagined him leaning against his kitchen counter the way he did, kicking the baseboard with one foot. "Stop worrying about the bakery and the apartment. I've already told you I'd hold it. Just let me make this one part of it easy for you."

"Why?" she asked, feeling odd about how indebted she already was to him. "We don't exactly have a long history together. You don't owe me anything this big."

"Because I can. Because it's the right thing to do and I'm able to do it." He must have realized the emotion showed in his voice, because he changed his tone to one that was more kidding and added, "So I have a hero complex. Sue me."

"Speaking of suing, have you decided what to do about the lawsuit yet?"

"I'm still working that out. Howard says the cookies will help me decide."

She laughed openly at that one. "He what?"

"He explained it to me twice," Cameron replied, laughing himself, "but I'm still not sure I understand it."

"That's Howard. Sounds like you've taken a shine to our illustrious mayor. Can't say I saw that coming. He's sure taking a shine to you."

"Trouble is, when Howard takes a shine to you, you end up managing hordes of volunteer cookie bakers for a project you're not even sure will succeed in the first place. There have to be easier ways to raise money than Cookie-grams. A good old-fashioned raffle perhaps. Car washes. Pony rides."

"If I were you, I wouldn't mention any of those around Howard. You might end up in charge of them all. Tell you what. You send me those real estate brokers' names, and I'll send you four no-fail cookie recipes. I'll even send them in large-batch versions, and I'll explain all the hard words for you. Consider it *Cookies for Cameron* instead of *Cookies for Dummies*."

"That'd be great. We'll stand a chance that way."

Suddenly, the urge to run back to Kentucky, to stand in her warm kitchen and listen to Howard's crazy volunteers baking all around her, to be part of the Cookiegram fund-raiser she'd called ridiculous a dozen times over, surged up inside her. A second ago she'd loved Cameron's idea of baking in her childhood kitchen, now it seemed such a poor substitute she could barely stand the notion. "You'll be fine," she said, almost choking up.

"So will you. Take care now and I'll call you when the flour settles."

After Dinah hung up, she walked into the kitchen and stared at the dull, ordinary white oven. *There are strangers in my kitchen, Lord!* Only which kitchen was hers now? I want to go home! Her heart cried out like a lost child. Only where was home now? The house she now owned, or the bakery and apartment Cameron Rollings owned and she only rented?

Life was so confusing and painful even two dozen batches of sticky buns couldn't make it better.

Cameron was in full-blown management mode.

Four recipes were typed up in large print, laminated and mounted on the four walls of the bakery. Four work-stations had been equipped with the needed ingredients. Taste and See was about to become the most efficient cookie factory Middleburg had ever seen. Managed by the soon-to-be locally licensed real estate mogul who would parlay his extraordinary community contribution into one launch of a dynamic local business. If the path to success and a street name change had to be paved with powdered sugar, then so be it.

Sandy and her five volunteers, shift one of three today, stood tying their aprons and awaiting his instructions. They looked a little frightened, actually. Maybe the clipboard and baking checklist was a bit much. Really, this was just cookies—perhaps he was investing a bit too much in this, banking too highly on the outcome. After all, what did it really matter if he couldn't manage to pull this off? It didn't reflect badly on him as a man, as a businessman or even as a broker. As a matter of fact, most of the people whose opinion he valued would have called him crazy for even attempting it in the first place, much less place any weight on his results.

"Who needs coffee?" he asked, remembering Aunt Sandy's warning that the gray-haired woman on the left was a bit foggy before noon.

"Oh, thank you," she said, walking toward the coffee station he'd set up in one corner. She seemed oblivious to the fact that her apron wasn't tied and fell off her waist with the first few steps.

"Let me help you with that." He picked the apron up off the floor and mentally reassigned her to a task not involving sharp objects. "You'll be breaking eggs this morning, Mrs. Carlson. You'll want that apron."

By noon, no less than twenty-two dozen sugar cookies had been baked and loaded onto wax paper flats. Success! When the more…um…skilled team came in at one-thirty, the trickier task of icing would begin. Cameron hoped he wouldn't be knee-deep in a sugar disaster by the end of the day.

As it turned out, Audrey Lupine had a way with piping royal icing and Aunt Sandy, working all three shifts today, showed herself to be the fastest icing spreader this side of the Mississippi. The other three ladies, evidently chosen for their superior skills, whipped their way through the assembly line of cookie decorating that Cameron had devised. Four designs on four kinds of cookies produced a respectable assortment of sixteen selections.

"The Keebler elves should watch their backs," Cameron mused as he surveyed the results so far. Contrary to his previous efforts at this, these cookies were actually attractive and, upon further inspection, surprisingly tasty. "Dinah would be proud of you," Cameron said to Sandy and her baking buddies as they loaded iced cookies into special boxes that would sit in Dinah's freezer—and other donated freezer space—until Cookiegram day.

Dinah's freezer. He supposed he might have to stop calling it that. But his brain still couldn't classify this as anything other than filling in for Dinah. Because he wanted her back. That's right—he missed loud, rambunctious, color-outside-the-lines Dinah Hopkins. He missed her vibrancy upending his life and that unnerved him. He'd always found elegant, conservative, powerful woman attractive. Now he found himself with a disturbing need to talk things over with an annoying redhead. Things like his huge, life-altering decision whether or not to sue Landemere.

"Dinah'd be proud of *you*, sugar," Sandy replied. "This is way out of your league and you handled it like a pro. Middleburg's going to owe you big time when this whole fund-raiser is over."

Cameron winked at his aunt. "Now you know you should never say those kinds of things to a deal maker like me. I'll find a way to take you up on them."

"That wouldn't surprise me in the slightest. And y'all done surprised me enough already in the month since you moved in." Aunt Sandy turned in a slow circle, taking in the bakery. "But land sakes, I sure do miss that girl. I can't imagine anyone else behind that counter but Dinah Hopkins."

Cameron finished wiping his hands on a dish towel and handed it to Audrey. She was taking all the towels and washcloths home to wash so that Cameron only had to run the industrial dishwasher when the day's work was done. "I was just thinking the same thing."

"Do you think she'll come back now that her mom is gone?" Audrey asked.

"That's between her and God," Sandy said. "But I've already told God what I'd like to see happen. I want that girl back here where she loves and is loved. But it ain't about what I want, or even what Dinah wants. It's about what God wants."

"I pray God wants her back in Middleburg." Audrey sighed. "And not just because the woman makes killer sticky buns. We'll miss her something fierce on the library board."

"We'll miss her something fierce in the choir," added Sandy. "We were short on altos even before she left."

Cameron thought, Why did I just know that woman was an alto? He'd never heard her sing. She probably had a silky, rich voice. Like that laugh of hers. It was a delight to hear it, even over the phone from miles away. It made him feel good to know he could make her laugh. Made him feel like a good guy, not the dark character who sat in his living room at night and contemplated legal revenge on the likes of Frank.

And that's when it hit him. Even though it was a complete turnaround from his previous thoughts, the moment it came to him, Cameron knew what he should do. Somehow Howard had been right; he'd know himself better by baking cookies. Sitting alone in his apartment, contemplating the ideological fallout of his actions was no way to decide his next course of action. He needed to craft the deal—talk face-to-face with the parties involved, to explore his options from the viewpoint of possibility, not the shadow of evil. He finished up, said goodbye to Aunt Sandy and her gang and flipped on his PDA to look at the coming weeks.

If they moved the fund-raiser just one week, he could pull

it off. There was enough time. It was tight, but it was worth
it. He had two more baking days to reach his goal. If he left
on Sunday and came back Wednesday, he'd have enough
time to visit the New York lawyers about the Landemere
case and still study for his real estate exam. He had time to
talk and explore and decide…and yes, he had time to make
a side trip to New Jersey to visit Dinah. He'd be able to tell
her how they handled…no, how they *mastered* the cookie
production and how much people missed her. He'd have the
chance to talk over his options with her and hopefully to help
her at a time when she really needed it. He'd somehow
convince Howard he needed one more week. Within minutes,
Cameron was upstairs buying an online ticket to the one
place he vowed he wouldn't return: New York.

Howard pulled up to the airport and put his car in park.
"You got your extra week. It better be worth it."

Cameron smiled. "When my Kentucky real estate license
comes through next month, I'll buy you a steak or something."

"You're a mover and a shaker, Rollings, that's for sure."
He looked straight at Cameron. "Believe or not, I respect
what you're doing now. I think this is the right choice." A
smug grin settled on his chubby face. "Didn't I tell you a
stint of cookie baking would lead you to a good decision?"

Cameron had doubts his tour of duty with flour and
sugar really had produced his decision to visit New York.
There was no telling Howard, however, when he'd decided
on the extent of his influence. "You did," he simply agreed.

"See if you can't use that extra week to get Dinah back
here. Tell her how much we all miss her," Howard said,
shaking Cameron's hand.

"I will."

Howard did not let go of Cameron's hand. "Right after you let her know how much *you* miss her."

Cameron did a double-take.

"What?" chuckled Howard, "You think I gave you that extra week just to chat with lawyers and bake cookies?"

Cameron still could not form a reply.

"Don't worry, son, I won't say a word to anyone. But remember, this is a small town full of women just itching to meddle. You won't get away with a secret like this for long. Especially if you convince that fine young woman to come back here where she belongs."

Cameron thought about denying it, but found it no use. "Start praying. And get the coots in on it." He grabbed his suitcase out of Howard's backseat.

"They've been in on it from the beginning, son. You don't fool an old coot for long. Vern's decided you're building a house up there on Lullaby Lane for more than just yourself."

"Yeah," Cameron said, leaning back through the window, "about that…"

"When you get back, we'll talk all about your big fancy plans for Lullaby Lane. You go figure out your future so's you can come on back here and make it happen."

"I'll try."

As he waited to check in, it dawned on Cameron that for the first time in his life he wasn't embarking on a *return* trip to New York. Sometime in the span of six weeks in Kentucky, his home had shifted. As if it sneaked out of the East Coast after dark and settled into the bluegrass region while he wasn't looking. He wasn't heading back home to New York. He was only visiting. Funny how Howard and Aunt Sandy and even kooky old Vern had figured it out before he had. Funny how God had known it way back when he set Cameron's path out of New York those months ago. Cameron remembered driving over the New York state line back then, thinking his life as he knew it was over. Well, that much was true. He just hadn't figured out yet how rich the new life just beginning would be.

"Going to or coming from?" the college student with too much eyeliner asked him as she settled into the airplane seat next to him.

Cameron just laughed, wondering what she'd think of him if he offered her one of the dozen overly frosted cookies in his carry on bag. "Both, actually."

Chapter Seventeen

Dinah tried to slow the thumping in her chest. "Monday night will work. I've got some accountant thing in the morning, but I'm free from two o'clock on." Cameron was in New York meeting with the case attorney. And he was asking to come here for a short stay after his meetings. Here. It was unfair what that did to her pulse.

"My train gets in at two-forty. I've booked two nights at the hotel on Seventh Street."

"Good choice. There's an outstanding bistro just down the block from it."

"Great. I know I'll be starved. I'll be too nervous to eat anything before my big meeting tomorrow."

"How can you be nervous about anything now? You got Howard to change his mind. You've achieved the impossible." Dinah hiked herself up to sit on the kitchen counter. "How are you—I mean about it all? Do you know what you want to do yet?"

She heard him exhale on the other end. "No, I'm trying not to make up my mind before I hear them out."

"That sounds smart. I think your gut will tell you what

to do once you get there. These kinds of things are always better done face-to-face." She wondered what kinds of things her stomach would do when she saw his face again. He had stuck with her, invaded her thoughts since their phone call a week ago. She'd think about how he pushed up his sleeves when he worked. The way he kept flicking his hair out of his eyes now that it had grown longer. When she'd tried out a new banana bread recipe yesterday, she'd caught herself wondering what he'd think of it—he'd said he didn't like bananas. "I'll be praying for you."

"I've moved the immovable Cookiegram. How can I go wrong?" He paused for a moment before adding, "That half—and most of the other half, too—told me to tell you how much they miss you."

Now there was a loaded sentence. Was he including himself in the contingent of Middleburgians who missed her? Did she even have business wondering something like that after how brief a time they'd known each other?

She was sure she'd felt something between them. There was a connection, there in the park when the world had been falling apart around her. It was just complicated by the worst possible timing. That and a couple of tons of emotional baggage like death, corruption, geography and the fact that she couldn't think straight about anything these days. As much as her intuition told her this guy was more than all his executive trappings, she didn't feel like she could trust her gut when it was tied up in such knots.

Cameron wasn't sure who he was expecting when he walked into the meeting the following Monday morning, but his first thought was how *normal* everyone looked. Without realizing it, in his mind he'd remembered the team of lawyers as a snarling monster. As though he'd walk into a room full of ready-to-pounce attorneys wringing their hands in vicious anticipation of bringing down their latest "bad guy." It was a ridiculous characterization, probably more born of his own internal conflict than anything they'd ever said to him. They were just a bunch of people doing their job—a job he'd first asked them to do—which is exactly what they looked like. Surprisingly, they also understood his own indecision.

Paul Sothington, the silver-haired calmly-speaking lead attorney who reminded Cameron a little too much of Howard Epson, folded his hands. "It sounds easy at first to launch something like this. Easy to classify this as 'clearly the right thing to do' until you're faced with the reality of it. This means resurrecting an unpleasant time in your life and it could be lengthy and messy. Everybody *admires* the whistle-blower, but no one understands more than we do how hard it is to find a job after it's all over." He leaned a little bit closer to Cameron. "This will just extend all that. I want you to proceed with your eyes open. It may end up costing you."

"It's already cost me," Cameron said. "I suppose I'm trying to figure out if it's worth costing me *more.*"

"We think it is," said an academic-looking woman at the end of the table. She wore glasses and had a stack of notes in front of her over an inch thick. "Or we wouldn't have agreed when you first came to us. There's too much grief for everyone in these things not to be careful. We'd never have advised going forward unless we saw a good shot at substantial results."

"Meaning?" Cameron had a picture of Frank making license plates in a dull gray jumpsuit. He'd be lying if he

didn't say it satisfied him on some level—Frank was fond
of six-hundred-dollar suits and four-hundred-dollar shoes.
One of Cameron's co-workers had taken to calling him
Grand Man because he calculated it took a thousand dollars
of clothing to get Frank out the door every morning.

"Meaning this case would set important precedents. As
I told you before, it's not just about how you lost your job.
It's about everyone who finds themselves in your shoes."
She wore an intense expression. "We wanted you to take
another look before you lost your chance to make that
impact. If we win this, we hand other attorneys the tools
they need to make it very hard for other companies to do
what Landemere did to you. I'm not saying Landemere
won't pay for what they did to you, but the lasting benefit
of this case will be the protection it gives all the other
people who have stood up against these shady deals. You
struck me as the kind of man who would care about that."

"Make no mistake," said a handsome younger lawyer
who looked like he'd just walked off a legal show on television—all driven and mussy-haired with searing eyes and
a sleek laptop. "Landemere will pay. If you want to watch
Frank and his cohorts go down, we take no prisoners."

The whole conversation made Cameron wonder: Was
there really such a thing as noble revenge? Or could you
simply never combine the two concepts? If he still felt
cravings for revenge, did he have any business dressing this
up as noble justice? "I've got some thinking to do. I'm sure
you understand that while I hate what happened to me, I'm
not in any hurry to prolong it. Right now I'd just as soon
never set foot in the same room as Frank ever again. I'm
happy not being in the same time zone as the man."

"We'll try to keep the trips down to a minimum," the

woman said, "but you will have to come to New York several times if we go forward and we can't guarantee what kind of stay you'll need to plan for during the trial if it comes to that. At the risk of asking a sore question, what is your current employment situation?"

Cameron thought of his short residency in Middleburg, balancing an insane baking timetable and the last of his real estate exam notes. Rather than answer "tycoot," he simply sighed and said, "I'm pursuing a self-employment scenario." It sounded so lame. As if in another minute he'd be selling carpet door-to-door out of the back of a rusty pickup truck.

The woman smiled. "That's good. That helps us a lot. And it may make it much easier on you."

Somehow Cameron didn't think "much easier" was really part of the picture. He certainly wasn't harboring any illusions that this would be "easy" if he chose to go through with it. Most likely, it wouldn't fall too short of ugly, and his only satisfaction would be knowing he did the right thing even when it was the much harder path.

Where was the simple answer when you needed it? The giant neon sign descending from heaven saying "This Way"? The chances of a pillar of fire descending on lower Manhattan were rather slim.

"May I suggest this?" Paul said. "Will you sign the release allowing us to access your personnel files and some other paperwork that will let us take our inquiry to the next level?"

"What will happen if I do?"

The younger man spoke up. "Well, most importantly, it will send Landemere a red flag that you're looking into legal action. If you were still living in the area or had close ties to the company, I'd let you know things might get a bit uncomfortable. They'll know we're looking deeper. Most of the time that makes everyone get especially civil, but occasionally it brings out the nasty side in people. I wouldn't go hanging out in the company watering hole if I were you."

The thought of sitting in any bar, restaurant, or even coffee shop with anyone from Landemere Properties was nearly repulsive. Cameron was finding his taste for the dark, cold, rush of Manhattan in general had soured fast. "No problem."

"But it will also let us get more information, do more planning, and we may be able to give you a clearer picture of what you're in for. Of course, it's still ultimately your call. You can keep the case dead, or we can keep talking."

Cameron took a second to gauge his gut response to that statement. No fight, no flight—mostly a cautious neutrality. It seemed safe to go ahead and explore further. He was sure he'd know more after talking the whole thing over with Dinah in a few hours.

"Okay. Take it to the next step. As long as I'm not committing one way or another yet."

The academic woman smiled softly. The young-gun lawyer looked victorious. Only Paul Sothington had the look that matched Cameron's gut: There's never a good day to launch a bloody war.

Dinah was unprepared for her dual reaction when she caught sight of Cameron in the crowd disembarking the commuter train. He was all business in his stunning charcoal gray suit—looking one-hundred-percent "tycoon." That part of him looked just like all the other cookie-cutter junior executives that had been half the reason she wanted out of the tristate area. Cameron looked handsome, but in an uninteresting kind of way if it weren't for the other touches—he wore a scarf striped with the Middleburg Mavericks team colors and carried a bakery box. She instantly suspected them to be a preview box of Middleburg charity Cookiegram cookies.

"The scarf's for you from Janet and Emily," he said by way of greeting. "I told them I wouldn't wear or carry flip-flops in the Maverick colors and I'm guessing you already have some anyway." He tossed the scarf so that it landed on her shoulders and she recognized just a hint of his cologne as the material hit her neck. She'd already received multiple gifts from both Janet and Emily, and she did in fact own flip-flops in the blue-and-white stripes of the Middleburg High School colors. Still, it was such a welcome gesture that a lump rose in her throat. Cameron smiled widely as he handed her the box of cookies and then moved around the car to put his luggage in her trunk. Sure enough, the box was topped by a Middleburg First Annual Charity Cookiegram card, signed "We Miss You!" by about two dozen people. Why had she not thought to use the waterproof mascara this morning?

When he got back in the car, Cameron pulled out a vintage-looking embroidered handkerchief. "Emily told me you'd need this. That woman knows her stuff." Which, of course, sent Dinah into open sniffles. "I have to say," he chuckled as she handed off the box and grabbed at the handkerchief, "I'm not sure if they miss you loads or if they're pulling out all the stops to bring you back."

"Probably both," Dinah sighed as she tried to dab her tears without smearing her mascara and search for a lady-like way to blow her nose. Both failed. "Oh, I was so determined to keep it all together when you got here."

"I came here to help, not to be awestruck at how well

you're managing. Do you want me to drive? I'm sure I can buy you a half hour of tear-soaked cookie consumption."

That made her laugh. As if she'd really stoop to eating all these on their way to dinner. Then again…she pulled at the strings and opened the box as he held it. She'd expected to find substandard but heartfelt cookies. Actually, when she was honest with herself, some part of her *wanted* to find substandard cookies. To know they couldn't quite pull it off without her.

They could. The collection of frosted cookies before her was downright admirable. Which made it impossible to explain to Cameron, who sat patiently holding a box of cookies in the passenger side of her car, why she started crying again. "They're so nice," she whimpered as she peered into the box.

"I will never take cookies for granted ever again. Those babies are harder than they look, even with the benefit of *Cookies for Dummies Like Cameron*."

Dinah selected a large pink heart and bit into it. Passable, but not the exquisite balance of butter and sugar she'd have been known for. The frosting didn't have enough vanilla and it was a bit on the thick side. The minor deficiencies gave her enough shallow satisfaction to stop crying. Which wasn't exactly noble of her, but she'd have to take what she could get under the circumstances. "Not bad, Rollings. I'm impressed."

He puffed up. "What do you mean 'not bad'? These are outstanding cookies. Fashioned with dedication from a volunteer force devoted to the greater good."

She laughed, which helped her catch her breath. "You sound like Howard."

Cameron impersonated the mayor. "I'll take that in the

complimentary spirit in which it *should* have been intended." It was dead on, which made her laugh harder.

"Now you really sound like Howard." She took another bite. The hard part was over. The sharp stab of missing Middleburg was ebbing against the warm enjoyment of seeing Cameron again. She wrapped the scarf around her neck and flexed her fingers against the steering wheel. "I'll save the rest of the cookies until after dinner. Hungry after your return to the big city?"

Cameron selected a cookie of his own before closing the box. "Starved."

Dinah had selected the Roundtree Bistro precisely because it didn't feel like any restaurant in Middleburg. It was what people called a "foodie" joint, full of exotic flavors, surprising spices and unique dishes that came in outrageous presentations. Dinah liked the food, was always amused by the presentation and the clientele, and could be assured it wouldn't remind her of Gina Deacon's Grill with Cameron across the table from her.

"Mercy!" she commented over her raspberry-pomegranate iced tea after hearing Cameron's account of the meeting. "It does sound like you're being asked if you want to start a war. Can they 'draft' you?" she added after thinking about it. "They can't make you open up the case, can they?"

Cameron leaned back in the booth. They'd managed to stay off the topic of his lawsuit through most of dinner, but she could tell he needed to talk it over, needed to process his responses to everything he'd heard this morning. She knew the feeling—how many times over the past few days had she wanted to launch into a story about her mother, only to edit herself because her companions might be uncomfortable talking about someone now dead?

"No. It's entirely my choice." He'd loosened his tie during dinner and now he undid it all together and slid it out from under his collar. The "off-duty executive" look—open dress shirt, jacket off, sleeves rolled up—suited him well. She liked him better in a turtleneck and blue jeans, but she had to say he still was a fine-looking man all citified and elegant. Okay, *really* fine. She usually didn't find the "dashing" look so…unsettling. He stirred his coffee and she could literally see the decision weighing him down.

"Will you? Change your mind and go through with it?"

Cameron leaned forward on the table. "I want it to be clear, you know? I don't want to decide this a third time. If I go forward with the case, I want to feel certain I'm taking the right path. But I don't feel certain either way—not at all. It's just murk on all sides. I get a little bit of vision here and there, a little sliver of clarity, and then *pow,* back into the murk again."

Dinah, her life reduced to a fistful of tasks on an index card, could relate. "Well, what's the last sliver of clarity you got?"

It took him a second to answer. "To come here." Even though he said it softly, she felt it pound into her chest.

"And how'd you get to that clarity?" she asked, trying hard not to sound flustered.

"You know, I think it was by baking cookies." On anyone else she would have described his expression as a twinkle in the eye. Somehow, she couldn't find the words for it on Cameron. Suddenly the powerful urge to get this man in her kitchen—to sift and stir things and make one recent happy memory in the New Jersey house—literally overtook her. She could no more explain it than she could resist it. "Well, then, I suppose we've got to bake." She stood up.

"Now?" he said, reaching for his wallet to settle the bill.

"You have a more pressing social engagement, Mr. Rollings?"

Chapter Eighteen

It could have been plucked from a thousand houses anywhere in the country. Dinah's mom's kitchen was the quintessential "Mom's kitchen," filled with experience and the tint of years. Half a dozen cookbooks stood on a shelf above the fridge—just where Cameron's mom kept hers. The dish towel hung over the oven handle, a trio of hot pads were held to the backsplash over the range with decorative magnets. The only distinction—and it was distinction enough—was the lack of photos on the fridge door. The fridge door in Cameron's parents' house was filled to the point of overload with photos, drawings from grandchildren, cards and invitations. Mrs. Hopkins's fridge door had only three occupants—a yellow-tinged photograph of a middle-aged man standing beside a boat—Dinah's dad, if the family resemblance was any indication, a photo of Dinah Cameron guessed to be from five years ago if not more, and a painfully large chart of pill dosages and treatment schedules. It made Cameron wonder if every fridge door so clearly reflected the lives of its owners. It made him irritated that his own fridge door was completely blank.

"Is this where you learned to bake?" he asked, slipping his coat over the back of a tasteful beige kitchen chair. The whole kitchen was very beige. Nothing at all like the riot of color and texture that was Dinah's kitchen back in Kentucky. It struck him with an odd sadness that he'd have to repaint over that riot if he got a new tenant.

"Not exactly. This is more like where I learned to make a mess. I did a lot of experimenting in the kitchen before I realized baking is as much science as it is art."

"You know, I get that now. It's math and formulas and procedures. Once I figured that out, it became a whole lot easier to get those cookies baked. I basically built a little factory."

"With a talkative and distractible production line?" Dinah teased as she flipped open the bakery box and ate another cookie. She'd eaten three on the way home from the restaurant. He thought that was a good sign. When they'd first met at the train station, it was hard to find the Dinah he knew hidden under the woman he saw. She was, at her core, a creature of joy. Take away the joy, and half the woman disappeared. It made him feel good to see glimpses of that joy return as they talked.

"Well, I didn't say it was easy. I just said it was eas*ier*."

"That's me," she said, running her hand down one of the potholders that hung over the stove. "It's not easy yet, but it's eas*ier*." She turned to look at him. "Someone said to me at the wake, 'You get past it, but you never get over it.' I think that's really true."

Cameron thought about his own ordeal. While it paled in comparison to Dinah's, he understood the idea. His life would be forever changed by what happened at Landemere and by what he chose to do from here. "My mom paints," he said, realizing he'd not shared much of his own family with her even though he knew lots about hers. "She says the same thing about color. When you mix a color, you can't ever take it back. You've got to move forward with the color you've just made, and your only choice is to keep adding to it if you don't yet have what you want." He shrugged, embarrassed to be waxing metaphorical all of a sudden. "It's dumb."

"No," she said, putting a hand on his elbow. "It's really smart. I like it." She let her hand rest there for a moment before giving it a little squeeze and turning toward the cabinets.

"It suits both of us, you know," she said with her head inside a cabinet under the sink. "Both figuring out…aha, there it is…"she pulled back out of the cabinet to reveal an enormous rolling pin, "where we need to go from here. What colors to mix in with the new color the world's just handed us. The trick," she stood up and handed the pin to him, "is remembering that God paints with *all* colors, if you don't mind my pushing the metaphor a bit."

Cameron grinned. She was always pushing metaphors more than just "a bit." And he couldn't help but smile at the memory of the first time he'd been in a kitchen late at night with Dinah Hopkins brandishing a rolling pin. "I don't mind." She began rummaging around the kitchen, pulling things out from the backs of cabinets, scouring the fridge, grouping ingredients on the countertop, selecting one tin while rejecting another. Again, slivers of the old Dinah. He had to say he felt better himself. Maybe baking really was the path to clarity.

"So what color are you going to choose now?" Dinah asked as she counted the eggs she'd just pulled from the refrigerator. He noticed she now wore a gold band on her right index finger and wondered if it was her mother's wedding band. "Do you feel up for the fight ahead?"

It was a useful question. "Yes and no. Yes, I think I'm strong enough to go through with it. But if I do, it has to be for the right reasons and right now, the only thing feeding that strength is a desire to watch Frank and his cronies fall."

"That's not true." She said it with an unsettling certainty. How could she know?

"What do you mean?"

Dinah pulled a large crockery bowl out from yet another cabinet and began dumping flour into it. No measuring spoons, no recipe, just handfuls of flour. More science than art?

"I mean if all you really wanted was to get this Frank character, you'd be waging war by now. Revenge is mostly an impatient business. Sure, you've got a tangle of motives in you, but come on, who doesn't?"

She stirred the flour with her hands, considered it for a moment, then added half a handful more. "Who didn't? Moses, David, Jacob—the Bible's full of guys with mixed motives. David was rather eloquent in his calls for revenge, if I remember. The man had enemies."

She looked up at him with an arched eyebrow. "Chocolate or peanut butter?"

"Huh?"

"Given our limited resources, you've got only two flavor choices. Chocolate or peanut butter?"

That wasn't even really a choice. "Chocolate."

She smiled. "Man after my own heart."

Cameron realized he wasn't really participating, just watching her bake, but that was fine with him. There was something completely mesmerizing about watching that woman in her element.

"You're thinking, praying, trying to figure out what God wants and how best you can honor Him." She pointed at Cameron with a white-dusted finger. "And you're forgetting that if you really are seeking to honor God, He'll honor whatever choice you end up making."

"Even if I choose to sue just to watch Frank squirm?"

"You won't, but if you did, I think God could do loads with that scenario. Pastor Anderson says we never learn half as much from the easy stuff as we do from the hard stuff." Her hand stilled for a moment, lying limp in the bowl. "I must be brilliant this month."

"It's that hard?" He wasn't doubting her—not for a moment—it was more like he was asking her to open up and talk about it.

She peeled the lid off the can of shortening and sent a dollop or two into the bowl. Not a calorie counter, this woman. Nor a big fan of watching fat content, either. "I'm trying to keep my head above water, but it just gets…harder." She'd started stirring and the spoon clanked harder against the bowl as she spoke. "More papers, more memories, more loose ends, more stuff to try and figure out what to do with." Her voice caught on the last few words.

It wasn't a conscious decision. It wasn't a gesture. It was more an impulse. He simply moved in and grabbed the spoon from her hand, taking up the stirring from where she left off. "Then let someone help out." It didn't matter that he almost whispered it, for he was right beside her now. "Community, remember? You taught me that."

She let her head fall against his shoulder and it felt as if his whole body had just been waiting for her. Cameron tried to get his breath back from the place it had run off to when she touched him. He had known girls for years, pursued a certain woman for months in college, yet never felt what just shot through him…what he realized had been shooting through him from the moment he met her. *Oh, Lord, don't be cruel enough to let me want this if I shouldn't have it. It'd be so easy to mess this up. To let it mess everything else up for both of us.* He closed his eyes as he stirred, unable to stop the moment from seeping into him, from changing him somehow. Something deep down settled into place— without asking permission but welcome on such an essential level he was powerless to refuse it.

"Come home." He'd tried not to say that even with all of Middleburg behind him wanting it. He was here to help her get through a tough time and he wanted badly to see her again, but certainly not to make demands or commands. Hadn't she had enough people in her life demanding she "come home"? She stiffened and he knew it for the misstep it was.

She pulled away and looked at him warily. "This is my home, Cameron. I was born here. This is my house now." Her words were low and clipped.

"Look, that was out of line, I know. It's just that…well, you're so…unhappy."

She shifted her weight onto one hip like she always did when she was angry. "My mother just died. I think I've got every right to be unhappy."

Cameron groaned, angry at his choice of words but still desperate to say what he was now feeling. "It's more than that. You have every right to be sad, to grieve. You lost your mom at the worst possible moment before you had a chance to put things right. I think what's happened to you is awful. It's unfair. It's tragic—and most things we use that word for hardly ever qualify, but this does." He walked away from the mixing bowl on the counter, away from her accusing eyes. "It's so obvious to me that you don't belong here that it's making me nuts to watch you try and convince yourself." He gestured around the bland kitchen. "This isn't you. Okay, it's your history, it's your childhood home, I get that. But it's not who you *are*. I stand in Taste and See and you're everywhere. Your touch is all over the color of walls and the way the customers stay and talk and the crazy-hued sugar bowls you use. Your wacky-colored personality is so inside my head that I had to come find you because I couldn't make this decision without talking to you." He froze, completely unaware of that fact until it leaped out of his mouth. He sunk against the wall, stunned. "Look, I don't know how it happened, but at some point I started needing you around. It may be for all the wrong reasons, but even that doesn't change that it's obvious staying here won't do you any good."

What did he just say? He needed her? Dinah's head was swimming—she was surprised, angry and more than a little taken aback by what she'd felt when she put her head on his shoulder. "And how do you know me well enough to say something like that?" she asked defensively.

He looked at her. "That's just it. I don't know you that well, so I don't have all the cartloads of emotional baggage you're dealing with. You know what I see when I look at this house? I see why you left. Taste and See is who you are and Taste and See can't happen here. Even if you painted this house eleven different colors, you don't belong in a nice, tidy suburb like this. You belong in Middleburg. I wouldn't need to know you a year to see that."

"How do I know I can't be here? When have I ever given

it a chance?" Dinah thought about the day she left, the defiance that practically flowed in her veins as she piled the few possessions she cared about in her car and drove out of her past. She'd thought that way once, that New Jersey couldn't ever hold her for long. Now the ache of her absence brought her nothing but a potent regret that clawed at her heart every moment since learning Mom was sick.

"You once told me," he replied, "that the one thing you were sure about in life was that God drew you to Middleburg." He took one step toward her and she felt herself bristle. "Your mom's death doesn't change that. The same God who drew you there drew you back here on His timing. Maybe…maybe all your mom needed was what she got. She didn't need you to come back and play the noble caretaker. She just needed to know that you would have. What if she just needed you to come home once, to be willing, and God knew that?"

That had to be wrong. There was so much left to repair, so many things to settle. The God she knew didn't take such shortcuts. "No." She stood there, unable to say more, until finally she stared at him and said, "Cameron Rollings, you are so far out of line…" She couldn't even finish the sentence.

"Yes, I'm out of line. Whatever motives got me on that plane may have been way out of line. I was out of line to delay the Cookiegrams, too. But the bottom line is, Dinah, I sat there and begged God to tell me what to do and all I kept hearing was 'go.' 'Go to her. Go to the lawyer.' I'm supposed to be here. I want to be here. Didn't you just say God could take a wrong motive and make a right thing happen from it?"

She did just make that argument to him. Why was God so skilled at turning her own words back on her? Still, she wasn't ready to accept any of what Cameron was saying. Right now, she wasn't sure she shouldn't call him a cab and tell him to go home. Wasn't he supposed to be helpful? That surely didn't include stirring up doubt and frustration and confusion.

"I make…*made* deals for a living. Let's look at the deal on the table for a minute."

Dinah bit back the wisecrack that was sitting on the tip of her tongue about making deals with the Devil. "What are you talking about?"

"Humor me for a minute, okay?"

She wasn't in the mood for this. As a matter of fact, she was feeling pretty exhausted all of a sudden.

"A minute," he pressed. The guy negotiated on instinct, like breathing.

"A minute," she relented.

"The whole point of a deal is about what each party brings to the table. What do you have that I need, what do I have that you need? Right? You need to grieve for your mother. And for that, in your own words, you need community. People around you who care about you. You don't have as much of that here as you do in Middleburg. Also, you wanted to buy the bakery in Middleburg before I bought it, didn't you?"

"You know I did."

"You need assets to buy a bakery. Has it occurred to you you're now standing in assets? Assets I could help you sell to turn around and buy the bakery?"

"From you? You just bought it yourself."

"Future details. But right now, I need a tenant. And Middleburg needs a baker. Emily needs a baker. Howard needs someone who can stand up to him." He stopped for a moment before adding, "I need you. I need you to help me get through this lawsuit without turning into someone I hate. All the people who would benefit from this lawsuit need you near me. And God must have known that, because He sent me to Middleburg just like He sent you. And now He sent me here with all the tools to bring you back."

On one level, Dinah couldn't have been more resistant to what he was saying. On another level, it made a perfect sort of sense. Not that it made any more sense out of how Mom died, but it put an odd harmony into everything. As if it were all pieces of a puzzle—some wonderful, some painful, but they all fit together in a whole. Which made it a lot like baking. Baking powder wasn't pleasant to taste, but it was a necessary ingredient. Flour wasn't tasty, but you couldn't bake without it. Sugar was tasty, but you couldn't eat it alone. She'd lost her mother, but before she died, God had managed to free her from the fight with her mother. Maybe Dinah never should have left, but she'd also found it within herself to return. Actually, she didn't find it within herself. It was a true work of the Holy Spirit— that transforming power to change a heart. She pulled the potholder off the wall and held it. "I don't know if I can bear to sell this place."

"If it's any comfort, I happen to know a lot about that whole leaving thing. I've got some experience ditching a painful past to do the whole risky future bit."

Dinah felt something uncurl in her soul. She'd wound this tight obligation around herself, as if staying in this house was a penance for her leaving it in the first place. But it wasn't leaving the house that mattered, it was leaving her mother, and God had repaired that. The reconciliation had been short-lived, but who was she to say that lessened its value? Could she get to the point where she saw it as God sparing Mom suffering instead of robbing Dinah of final goodbyes?

Would she even be considering it if Cameron Rollings hadn't moved heaven and earth—and Cookiegrams—to be standing in her kitchen, daring to say things she didn't want to hear?

Cameron was suddenly beside her. "I care about you. I can help you. And you can help me." He touched her chin. "Community."

She looked at him, at his tender eyes that held the same struggle she now knew, and realized that God had not only pulled her to Middleburg, but pulled him as well. Pulled them together before they even knew they needed each other. She did need him. It was okay to admit that. She needed Middleburg and that didn't make her a traitor to her mother's memory. She felt a sensation of release. Not of release away from something, as she had felt that day she left New Jersey, but release toward something.

Toward someone. She let her head fall on his shoulder again and all the pieces fit together. She didn't need to leave New Jersey right away, but she needed to leave. "Only I could pull off something like running away from home by coming home."

Cameron put one hand on her cheek and turned her face up toward his own. "You're a frighteningly complicated woman, Dinah Hopkins."

It sounded so amazing when he said her name. The release in her soul settled into something more intimate. "You're not exactly simple yourself."

She lost herself searching his dark eyes for a long

moment. Then, moving his other hand around to the small of her back, he took a deep breath and asked, "Would it be totally inappropriate to kiss you right now?"

Dinah grinned and settled into the amazing strength of his arms. "Totally. But do it anyway."

Chapter Nineteen

It must have been something like two in the morning. Cameron had every reason to feel wiped, but kissing Dinah gave him such a rush he thought he could take on the world. Sure, it was an extraordinary kiss and he'd be lying if he said he hadn't thought about what it would be like to kiss her any number of times since their embrace at the mailbox the day she left, but it was so much more than that. Half the stuff he'd said to her tonight he'd barely figured out as it left his mouth. As if the ideas weren't even his own. It felt like such a corny thought to believe that God really had drawn them together, but then again, it was the oldest thought in the universe. Who was God if not capable of such things? Who could redeem such misguided motives and tragic circumstances but God? It made every sense and no sense at all, but Cameron found himself at such peace he couldn't begin to sleep—which, he thought to himself as he looked at the pale orange numbers on the hotel room clock, makes no sense, either.

Lord, he sighed into the darkness, *I'm so lost here. I think I've found the path You want me to take, but it's so far from what I thought I was doing. When I left New York. When I left Kentucky. I'm going to have to lean completely on You, because I haven't the foggiest idea how to play this from here.*

But he did. The strangest thing of all was that Cameron knew exactly what to do from here. It was just so outrageous he could barely accept it as the wisest option. In the last eight weeks all his ideas of plans and career paths, his concepts of right and wrong had been twisted into knots. For the first time in his adult life—the life he'd built upon his sharp skills and sound reasoning—Cameron realized he couldn't trust his own judgment. *You're going to have to take it from here, Lord. I can't begin to say where You're taking me, but maybe that's the point.* He smiled to himself. *That is the point, isn't it? I'm sitting here worried if I can take on the legal battle, but I can trust You in that. I'm unsure what will happen with Dinah, but I can trust You in that, too, can't I? I'm only beginning to guess why You've got me in Kentucky, but Your reasons are trustworthy. You've got the better plan, so it's okay if I can't grasp mine yet.*

Cameron thought about all the people praying for Dinah. He'd spent the last year building a career, doing all the right things, but Dinah had spent the last year building a life—even if some people felt it was doing all the wrong things. For both of them, the past year had become a jumbled mix of running away and coming home. To the point now where he could no longer say which was which.

But I'm sure of her, Lord. Of the person I am when I'm with her. Even if he couldn't tell what the future would hold for them, he knew that right here, right now, they were meant to be together. He had strengths she needed and she gave him boldness he hadn't realized he'd lost. *You knew, didn't You Lord? You knew all along. And even if I don't know what to do next, You do. You always will.*

Cameron must have fallen asleep at some point because the next thing he knew, his cell phone went off and he opened his eyes to see daylight seeping through the hotel curtains. He groped around the unfamiliar nightstand until his hand found the phone and flipped it open. "Hello?"

"Hey, sleepyhead. It's past seven. I've been up for hours."

Dinah's voice was a cascade of low husky tones. He really did need to hear her sing one of these days. He was sure he'd find it irresistible. "Good morning to you, too."

"Not a morning person?"

He squinted into the sunlight. "In my defense, it is six in the morning Kentucky time."

"Well, then, I'm glad I didn't call at six like I wanted to." She chuckled, and even half-asleep, it rumbled down his spine.

"Thanks for that." He sat up and found his glasses. "How are you?"

"I'm starving. Uncle Mike is, too. So we're going to meet for breakfast."

"We?" Cameron was so tired he was finding even the cheap in-room coffeemaker suitable for instant caffeination.

"I want you to meet Uncle Mike. He's going to help me decide what to do about the house. And after breakfast, I want you to come with me to the real estate office."

Forget the in-room coffee, Cameron was fully awake now. "Real estate."

If you could hear someone smile over the telephone, Cameron heard Dinah smile. "Yep. I'm ready to consider selling the house. I haven't decided for sure yet, but I'm okay with talking to someone. If you'll help."

"Count on it."

"We'll pick you up in twenty minutes?"

He was already fumbling through his case for his razor. "Make it fifteen."

It was a clear February day—brisk, but with a stunning wash of sunshine. Dinah squinted one eye, shot and sent the basketball sailing through the old rusty hoop still hanging above her mom's garage door. "I was so sure I'd have to rush it to market, clear it out faster than I was ready to."

"Nah," Cameron said as he caught the ball and dribbled up for his own shot. Dinah sat back on her heels and smiled. There was no competition this time; no showing off or showing him up, just a delightful companionship she'd always known could be between them. "Prime residential season doesn't really start until March anyway. Even then, this is a good market for a home like this. You can take your time—even wait until April if that's what you need." He missed his shot, grinned at her and shrugged.

Dinah glanced around the yard. The trees she climbed as a kid, the garden her mom started the year Dad died, the deck they'd grilled on after the parade every Memorial Day. "This yard is really gorgeous in April. All the buds." She felt that familiar surge of nostalgia, but with a warmth, not a pang. She'd condensed her relationship with her mother down to the last tense years, but there were decades of good memories as well. There was a whole life there, not just one extended argument. She really was making peace with her mother's memory. With her passing.

Cameron looked up at her, paused and palmed the ball as he walked toward her. "She's here."

"She's everywhere." Dinah teared up, but in a good way. "But I don't think I have to be here anymore. I'm not ready to let it go today, but I'm ready to let it go a little while from now." She took Cameron's hand and led him toward the backyard. "This yard should have a pack of kids running through it. There should be a mess of bikes piled up in the garage and a dog barking at the back door. Mom would like there to be life in this house again." She looked at Cameron, his dark hair shining in the sunlight, the collar of his coat all messed up from shooting baskets. "She'd have liked you, I think. Especially back when you were a citified, stuffy old broker."

He pulled her to him, "And now that I'm Middleburg's most promising young coot?"

She eyed him critically, feeling the long-lost playfulness come back to the edges of her spirit. "Well, that remains to be seen."

One dark eyebrow went up. "Why?"

"We have unbaked cookies to tend to, mister. I need to assess those budding baking skills of yours."

"Oh," he started toward the kitchen. "But that's my secret; I don't bake. I'm management. I only supervise."

Dinah took one hand and ran it along his jaw line as she used the other hand to calmly snatch the ball away from him. "So supervise me." With that, she ran toward the back door, feeling the energy and balance and God's marvelous pleasure as she made for the kitchen.

Cameron smiled as the cab turned onto Ballad Road, still thinking about how Dinah soundly kissed him goodbye at the airport, promising to pack up and return in about a week. It would, he guessed, be the first of many Kentucky–New York–New Jersey shuttles for both of them. He'd decided on the plane that he would go forward with the lawsuit. The decision had settled peacefully on him and he felt God's protection despite the challenges that lay ahead.

As he got out of the cab, Emily Montague practically tackled him in a hug. "You've brought her home! Thank you!" she said.

He laughed at her exuberance. "You know Dinah well enough to know no one tells that woman what to do. Besides," he said as he paid the driver and pulled his suitcase from the back of the cab, "I think God is the one bringing her home. I just helped her to see a few things, that's all."

Emily crossed one arm over the other and gave him a look. "I can just imagine."

Had the whole world figured out their feelings before they did? Was this what he was in for in Middleburg, the whole town knowing his business? After Manhattan's anonymity, this was going to take a whole lot of getting used to. "We didn't really settle anything for certain, Emily. I wouldn't get all excited just yet."

"Oh yes, I can. Dinah called me an hour ago to say she'll bake my wedding cake. In her own bakery. Well, I suppose I should say in the bakery she rents from you, but you know it'll always be Dinah's bakery in my mind."

Always be Dinah's bakery. He did like the sound of that. And Emily was actually tearing up over it. "Sorry," she said, blushing and wiping away a tear with her mitten. "I'm just so happy. I couldn't bear not having her around."

Cameron wanted to say, "Me, too," but he stuck with a much safer "I know."

"Not only that, but she says I have you to thank for all the extra time she has to work on it. It seems more than half the Cookiegram cookies are in the freezer stocked up and ready to go, thanks to you."

He was insanely proud of those cookies. He'd started the whole project just to get on Howard's good side, but it had turned into so much more. Already, after less than two months in Middleburg, he knew more people by name than he ever had outside of his office in New York. And to top it all off, when he'd turned on his phone after the plane landed, he'd had a voicemail from a guy from church, asking if Cameron wouldn't like to come join a pickup basketball game on Saturday mornings.

"Welcome home," Emily called as she turned and started up the street toward her shop.

"Thanks." And he was home, wasn't he? He stood for a moment, looking around the charming little town, up the street where he could already name four out of five shop owners, and breathed it all in. There, standing in the sunlight, he caught a glimpse of what Dinah always talked about; how she could be so sure God had brought her here. Even with the lawsuit question settled, lots of other things were still up in the air. But he had a place and people to help him solve it all. That whole community thing Dinah always pushed. He understood it now and maybe that had been God's plan all along.

Waving at "Mac" MacCarthy in the office next door, Cameron left his luggage in the apartment foyer and went into the bakery. He flipped on the lights and sighed. He'd found the place so odd the first time he saw it—now it was so achingly bare without all those oddities. Because all the oddities were Dinah. Her style, her joy, her energy. He found Dinah's little sign that said "Back in a Minute" still sitting on the counter. *Thank You,* he prayed as he pulled the bakery door shut behind him. *I couldn't bear to see anyone else in this space but her.*

I'm in love with her. It struck him as he dragged his luggage up the stairs to his apartment, making him stop and stand for a moment in the middle of the stairway. I am. I'm in love with Dinah Hopkins. He should tell her. But how?

Well, now, there really was only one way to tell her, wasn't there? Before he even got to the top of the stairs, he pulled out his cell phone and called up Janet Bishop at the hardware store.

Dinah closed the top of the shipping crate, feeling the thud deep in her heart. She and Uncle Mike had spent the last five days sorting items from her mom's house between a garbage bin, Uncle Mike's van and a crate bound for Middleburg. Together they watched the crate being loaded onto the truck that would begin its journey to Kentucky as Dinah flew back to Middleburg. It had been a healthy process for the two of them. They'd chatted and reminisced as they went through the house to find the items they wanted to keep, while clearing out other items that needed to be discarded. An emotional decluttering as much as a practical one. Some of it made them laugh—like the sixteen pairs of black patent leather pumps, which brought a barrage of teasing from Uncle Mike about Dinah's extensive flip-flop wardrobe. Some of it, like a set of war letters from her dad to her mother wrapped carefully in lace and tied with a lavender ribbon, made them cry. They found box after box of Dinah's college and high school artwork in Mom's attic—she'd kept so many pieces, even the ones Dinah thought the craftsmanship of was definitely substandard. Another box contained newspaper clippings from Dinah's basketball days. All the classic "mom" hoarding underscored the truth Dinah was coming to understand—despite their friction, they really did love each other.

Uncle Mike clasped his arm around Dinah's shoulder. "We'll attempt another box when you come back in March. Shannon and I will look after the house until then. Maybe even start some of those repairs the real estate broker suggested." Cameron had hooked them up with a wonderful, compassionate broker who had helped Dinah and Mike lay out a plan for emptying the house, making a few important repairs and upgrades and putting it on the summer market. With that plan set, Dinah could freely turn her attention back to Middleburg.

And the man waiting for her there when she flew back today, Valentine's Day of all days. How many times had Cameron crossed her mind in the past two days? How many times had she sent up a prayer of thanks for who he was, how he'd come into her life and what he'd come to mean to her? When she'd read those letters between her parents, between two people who could hang on to what they felt about each other even though the future was drastically uncertain, it felt like God was showing her what was possible between her and Cameron. Was it love? As reluctant as she was to admit it, Dinah was coming to think that it was. Yep, she might very well be in love with the last person on Earth she'd suspect. Wouldn't Emily enjoy that one?

Dinah swallowed the lump in her throat as the truck pulled out of the driveway. "Well, Patty," said Uncle Mike, his own voice a bit wobbly, "Happy Valentine's Day.

You're finally going to Kentucky. Godspeed, little sister." She and her uncle stood silently for a moment, saying one of the many goodbyes they'd say to all of Patty Hopkins's earthly possessions. It was an odd, bittersweet sensation.

They were about to head over to Uncle Mike's when a white delivery truck pulled up. Dinah and her uncle caught each other's eye as a young woman got out of the truck and headed up the walk with a square white box in her hand.

"Valentine package for Dinah Hopkins?"

Dinah calculated that only a handful of people would know to mail something to her here. "Yes?"

The woman held the box and an electronic pad out to Dinah. "Sign here."

Dinah handed the box off to her uncle and signed the pad. "Who in the world is Ty Coot?" Uncle Mike asked, squinting at the label.

Dinah's heart did a slam dunk. "What?"

"The box is from a Ty Coot back in Middleburg. Who's he?"

Dinah practically grabbed the box out of her uncle's hand. Sure enough, the box held a certain man's Ballad Road address with the name "Tycoot" above it." She worked off the packaging to reveal a box identical to her earlier Cookiegram from her friends in Middleburg. Only this time the card on top was a big red heart with a single name: Cameron. She pulled at the string and flipped open the lid. And stared. And sank down to sit on the front steps of her mother's house in joyful awe.

A dozen bright red frosted heart cookies gazed out at her. Cookiegrams were just supposed to have a personalized telegram card on top of the box, but someone had taken things a step further. These cookies were actually frosted with a personal message: "I LOVE YOU," carefully, yet obviously inexpertly, written out in white icing. Some of them had turned out downright laughable, and yet they were the most beautiful confections Dinah had ever seen.

"He loves me," she nearly whispered, lifting a cookie from the box.

"Who loves you?" Uncle Mike sat down beside her and peered into the box. "Ty Coot?"

"Cameron."

The smile on her uncle's face told her he'd already guessed who "Tycoot" was. "Can't say I didn't see that coming."

She looked at him, feeling a tear sneak down her face. "You knew?"

He grinned and kissed her forehead. "You didn't?" He pulled her into a big hug, just like he used to when she was small.

"Oh, Uncle Mike," Dinah said as she hugged him with all her might. "I love him back."

He pulled her back to arms length as his smile broadened. "Does he know?"

"Not yet," she said, "but my plane lands at four, and you know what today is."

It was so cheesy. Cookies. The airport. Valentine's Day. Why had he sent the box, knowing he could have told her face-to-face now? She hadn't called or responded. He'd intentionally not left her much time to do so, timing the delivery to give her an emotional boost just as she went through the difficult task of actually leaving—or so he thought. It seemed brilliant at the time, he thought to himself. He couldn't remember the last time he felt so utterly vulnerable. For a deal maker, this was murder—the other side held all the cards. *Save me, Lord,* Cameron prayed as he stood at the baggage claim with his heart stomping around beneath his ribs. He scanned the stream of passengers coming down the hallway for her red hair, absurdly listening for the sound of flip-flops. He'd know her response just by the way she walked.

A red head bobbed up out of the crowd. No face, just a ponytail surfacing momentarily in the sea of heads. It re-appeared further down the throng, off to the left.

She was running. Trying to jump up to see. That had to be good, right?

Ten feet down the hallway she popped up again, still not high enough for him to catch her face. Come on Dinah, show off some of those basketball skills of yours. Jump! He was moving toward her, but the crowds weren't really allowing him the chance to come much closer. Who knew a small city airport could get so crowded?

Finally, after what felt like hours but must have been only seconds, she moved into sight. Her face said it all as she scanned the room and Cameron heaved an instanta-neous prayer of thanksgiving.

The ten feet between them became a marathon of dodging and weaving until Dinah threw herself into his arms. He pulled her up off the ground into his embrace. She loved him! He wasn't in this alone. He'd never been in this alone, even from the first. He kissed her until she giggled, then he set her down and held her face in his hands and kissed her again.

"Me, too," she said, grinning wildly.

"Aw, nice going, cookie boy," came a gravelly voice from his left. Cameron tore his gaze away from his gorgeous redhead to see a short, spunky woman with gray hair and half-moon reading glasses winking at him. The woman turned to Dinah. "Definitely a keeper."

Dinah rolled her eyes and blushed. "Cameron, this is Josie. She sat next to me on the plane."

Josie winked again. "And heard the whole story."

"I was a bit nervous on the flight."

"She talks a lot when she's nervous, this one." Josie touched her finger to her ear and wiggled it and Cameron suspected more than just altitude had taxed the old woman's ears. "But it was easier to humor her on a day like today." She smiled, shrugged indulgently at the two of them, and went off with the rest of the passengers.

Dinah talked the whole way home, making dreamy little sighing noises in between bursts of moving, packing and house-selling updates. Cameron felt a zing every time she caught his eye and seemed unable to stop his hand from sneaking off the steering wheel to clasp hers. He'd seen his dad do it a million times to his mom—sneak his hand across the couch or the car or the kitchen table, always marveling at the expression that came over his dad's face. Always, somewhere in the back of his mind, hoping that feeling would come to him. And it had. He was in love. And it felt like it could last a lifetime. He could picture it—his hand sneaking across the kitchen table to catch hers twenty-five years from now. The swell of affection and satisfaction in his chest seemed almost unbearable. This was it. *She* was it.

Dinah's sighs turned to a teary-eyed silence as he put his keys in the lock and opened the bakery door. She picked up the Back in a Minute sign from the counter and held it to her chest. "I'm home," she said as Cameron put his arms around her.

"I am, too. Happy Valentine's day, Dinah," he said, and kissed her again, just because it felt so wonderful right there, where he was, in the Taste and See Bakery in Middleburg, Kentucky.

Chapter Twenty

"Fourteen thousand, eight hundred and twelve." Janet looked up from her calculator at the table by the bakery door. "I'd never have believed it. Maybe that extra week of orders gave us just the boost we needed. We made it."

"Well," said Audrey Lupine, "close enough."

"I think we can all congratulate ourselves on a job well done," Aunt Sandy said, looking straight at Cameron. The Town Council, the Community Fund Board and all the volunteers had packed into Taste and See for a "count up the proceeds" party. Which meant that everybody who was anybody in Middleburg was in the room. Cameron took a deep satisfaction that he could identify half the room by name. He was exhausted—most of them were from the last-minute box-a-thon it took to get all those goodies packed up and labeled for the high school seniors to deliver today.

He'd received two boxes today. One Cookiegram came from Aunt Sandy—from his parents, actually, via Aunt Sandy—a box of yellow-frosted stars with the message "WELL DONE!" on the telegram card. The other was a box of specially red frosted hearts with "I LOVE YOU,

TOO." That one didn't have a telegram label because it didn't need one.

"I'm so glad we got to have Dinah do both the cookies and our wedding cake," Emily said.

"Not just me," corrected Dinah. "I'd never have been able to do all these cookies alone. Good thing Cameron saw to the volunteer brigades to expand my staff."

"But it's just you on my wedding cake." Emily looked concerned. "You're not having volunteers do that?"

"No, honey, it'll be highly trained professionals," Dinah assured her.

Cameron was more than happy to be added to the guest list for this upcoming wedding. He was thrilled to be Dinah's date for the occasion—not only would he get to see her finest creation in the amazing cake, but rumor had it he might get to hear her sing. He was itching for the chance to get that woman out on the dance floor, too. It was going to be a heartwarming celebration and he was glad to be part of it.

"Oh now, don't pout Howard," Dinah came out from behind the counter. "We'll make your big ol' goal yet." She pulled a slip of paper out of her back pocket. "How much do we need, Janet?"

"One hundred eighty-eight dollars," Janet and Howard said simultaneously.

Dinah grinned. "Well, now isn't it interesting, then, that I have here a two-hundred-and-fifty-dollar check given to me by my uncle Mike. A collection from the friends and family of Patty Hopkins. And ain't it amazin'," she applied her trademark twang, "that Uncle Mike asked me to look for a charitable contribution to make in my dear mama's name."

"Dinah, that's so sweet," Sandy said. "But maybe you

want to plant a tree or something. We're more than fine with what we made," she leveled a glare at Howard, "aren't we?"

Cameron watched Dinah's eyes narrow. That woman was up to something.

"Oh, but I *am* planting something. Something lasting. You might even say it's a watershed moment." Dinah walked over to Howard. "Your honor, I am prepared to sign this check over to the Cookiegram fund right here in front of all these witnesses, if you'll just grant me the tiniest favor."

Howard's reply was a look of suspicious amusement. "And what's that?"

"Sonata Lane." She waved the check in front of him, grinning. Cameron felt his heart gallop.

"You mean…" Howard started.

"I do in fact mean Middleburg's first-ever street name change."

"Well, it's not really my decision now, is it? There are procedures to be followed. The preservation task force might need to…"

"Oh no," chimed in Emily, currently arm-in-arm with her husband-to-be. "I must say I've come around to Dinah's way of thinking."

Cameron started having trouble breathing calmly.

"Audrey," Dinah said, her voice smooth and silky, "how many do we need for a quorum of the zoning board?"

"Five. I just happened to look it up this afternoon." Audrey's grin rivaled Dinah's.

Aunt Sandy jumped on the bandwagon. "Raise your hand if you're on the zoning board." Four hands went up. "And you make five, Howard. Isn't that handy?"

"Astonishing," said Howard, just barely starting to grin.

"I move," said a man Cameron had met in the hardware

store only yesterday, "that we call an impromptu meeting of the Middleburg planning and zoning commission for the sole purpose of considering the name change of the Route 26 extension, commonly known as Lullaby Lane."

"Second," said Vern Murphy, smiling broadly.

Howard looked around the room, caught Cameron's eye with a shrug that made everyone laugh and said, "All those in favor?"

"Aye!"

The room burst into applause. "Well, Cameron Rollings, you got your Kentucky license and you got your precious name change. So pretty soon son, I expect to see you out there sellin' every house you build on…" he took a deep breath and rolled out the words, "Sonata Lane."

Cameron caught Dinah's hand and pulled her to him. He took the check she held out, handed it to Howard without taking his eyes off his amazing woman and kissed her. "All but one."

* * * * *

Christmas comes to horse country in
BLUEGRASS CHRISTMAS
Allie Pleiter's next Steeple Hill Love Inspired®
On sale September 29, 2009
from Steeple Hill Books.

Dear Reader,

I'm definitely more about snacking than baking, but even I know how much God loves surprise ingredients in our lives. Events that feel like endings are often beginnings, and God delights in taking our lives in new directions with unexpected companions. Dinah and Cameron discover that God knows just how to combine two people who haven't yet discovered how much they need each other. Together, they learn the value of community and the trustworthiness of God's path—even when you can't see where your steps are leading. It's my prayer that their story offers you encouragement in your own life and increases your own trust in God's plan. And if I've inspired you to send some cookies to someone you love, then by all means, get baking! As always, I love to hear from you at alliepleiter.com or P.O. Box 7026, Villa Park, IL 60181. (Please don't send cookies…I'm doing enough sit-ups as it is!)

DISCUSSION QUESTIONS

1. What would you have done about Frank's crimes in Cameron's shoes? Do you think the high stakes involved would alter your decision?

2. Do you think what Sandy Burnside did was ethical or questionable?

3. Why do family estrangements like Dinah's happen? What can be done about it?

4. Was Dinah's only choice to move back to New Jersey? Is there another way you might handle the situation in her place?

5. If you were Patty Hopkins's friend, what would you have suggested she do regarding her relationship with Dinah?

6. Baking serves as a comfort to Dinah. What serves as a comfort to you? Do you get enough chances to do it? How can you change that if you don't?

7. Was Howard right or wrong to push Cameron into his role managing the cookie baking?

8. Have you ever paid a high price for doing the right thing? How has that experienced changed you?

9. Dinah talks a lot about community. What's your definition of community? Do you have a community around you?

10. Would you have sued if given the chance Cameron had?

11. Is Middleburg right or wrong to resist change the way it does? What does it gain by resisting? What does it lose?

12. Is there someone in your life you've lost contact with for regrettable reasons? What can you do about restoring that relationship? What's God's role in that situation?

Dumped via certified letter days before her wedding, Haley Scott sees her dreams of happily ever after crushed. But could it turn out to be the best thing that's ever happened to her?

Turn the page for a sneak preview of
AN UNEXPECTED MATCH
by Dana Corbit,
Book 1 in the new
WEDDING BELLS BLESSINGS *trilogy,*
available beginning August 2009
from Love Inspired®

"Is there a Haley Scott here?"

Haley glanced through the storm door at the package carrier before opening the latch and letting in some of the frigid March wind.

"That's me, but not for long."

The blank stare the man gave her as he stood on the porch of her mother's new house only made Haley smile. In fifty-one hours and twenty-nine minutes, her name would be changing. Her life as well, but she couldn't allow herself to think about that now.

She wouldn't attribute her sudden shiver to anything but the cold, either. Not with a bridal fitting to endure, embossed napkins to pick up and a caterer to call. Too many details, too little time and certainly no time for her to entertain her silly cold feet.

"Then this is for you."

Practiced at this procedure after two days back in her Markston, Indiana, hometown, Haley reached out both arms to accept a bridal gift, but the carrier turned and deposited an overnight letter package in just one of her hands.

Haley stared down at the Michigan return address of her fiancé, Tom Jeffries.

"Strange way to send a wedding present," she murmured.

The man grunted and shoved an electronic signature device at her, waiting until she scrawled her name.

As soon as she closed the door, Haley returned to the living room and yanked the tab on the paperboard. From it, she withdrew a single sheet of folded notebook paper.

Something inside her suggested that she should sit down to read it, so she lowered herself into a floral side chair. Hesitating, she glanced at the far wall where wedding gifts in pastel-colored paper were stacked, then she unfolded the note. Her stomach tightened as she read each hand-written word.

"*Best? He signed it best?*" Her voice cracked as the paper fluttered to the floor. She was sure she should be sobbing or collapsing in a heap, but she felt only numb as she stared down at the offending piece of paper.

The letter that had changed everything.

"Best what?" Trina Scott asked as she padded into the room with fuzzy striped socks on her feet. "Sweetie?"

Haley lifted her gaze to meet her mother's and could see concern etched between her carefully tweezed brows.

"What's the matter?" Trina shot a glance toward the foyer, her chin-length brown hair swinging past her ear as she did it. "Did I just hear someone at the door?"

Haley tilted her head to indicate the sheet of paper on the floor. "It's from Tom. He called off the wedding."

"What? Why?" Trina began, but then brushed her hand through the air twice as if to erase the question. "That's not the most important thing right now, is it?"

Haley stared at her mother. A little pity wouldn't have been out of place here. Instead of offering any, Trina snapped up the letter and began to read. When she finished, she sat on the cream-colored sofa opposite Haley's chair.

"I don't approve of his methods." She shook the letter to emphasize her point. "And I always thought the boy didn't have enough good sense to come out of the rain, but I have to agree with him on this one. You two aren't right for each other."

Haley couldn't believe her ears. Okay, Tom wouldn't have been the partner Trina Scott would have chosen for her youngest daughter if Trina's grand matchmaking scheme hadn't gone belly-up. Still, Haley hadn't realized how strongly her mother disapproved of her choice.

"No sense being upset about my opinion now," Trina told her. "I kept praying that you'd make the right decision, but I guess Tom made it for you. Now we have to get busy. There are a lot of calls to make. I'll call Amy." Trina dug the cell phone from her purse and hit one of the speed dial numbers.

Haley winced. In any situation, it shouldn't have surprised her that her mother's first reaction was to phone her best friend, but Trina had more than knee-jerk reasons to make this call. Not only had Amy Warren been asked to join them downtown this afternoon for Haley's final bridal fitting, but she also was scheduled to make the wedding cake at her bakery, Amy's Elite Treats.

Haley asked herself again why she'd agreed to plan the wedding in her hometown. Now her humiliation would double as she shared it with family friends. One in particular.

"May I speak to Amy?" Trina began as someone answered the line. "Oh, Matthew, is that you?"

That's the one. Haley squeezed her eyes shut.

* * * * *

*Will her former crush be the one
to mend Haley's broken heart?
Find out in AN UNEXPECTED MATCH,
available in August 2009
only from Love Inspired®.*

Love Inspired

Even their meddling mothers don't think practical single dad Matthew Warren and free-spirited nanny Haley Scott are right for each other. But they surprise everyone—including themselves—by proving that opposites do attract!

Look for

An Unexpected Match

by
Dana Corbit

WEDDING BELL *Blessings*

Available August wherever books are sold.

www.SteepleHill.com

Steeple Hill®

REQUEST YOUR FREE BOOKS!

2 FREE INSPIRATIONAL NOVELS
PLUS 2
FREE
MYSTERY GIFTS

YES! Please send me 2 FREE Love Inspired® novels and my 2 FREE mystery gifts (gifts are worth about $10). After receiving them, if I don't wish to receive any more books, I can return the shipping statement marked "cancel". If I don't cancel, I will receive 4 brand-new novels every month and be billed just $4.24 per book in the U.S. or $4.74 per book in Canada. That's a savings of over 20% off the cover price. It's quite a bargain! Shipping and handling is just 50¢ per book.* I understand that accepting the 2 free books and gifts places me under no obligation to buy anything. I can always return a shipment and cancel at any time. Even if I never buy another book, the two free books and gifts are mine to keep forever.

113 IDN EYK2 313 IDN EYLE

Name	(PLEASE PRINT)	
Address		Apt. #
City	State/Prov.	Zip/Postal Code

Signature (if under 18, a parent or guardian must sign)

Mail to Steeple Hill Reader Service:
IN U.S.A.: P.O. Box 1867, Buffalo, NY 14240-1867
IN CANADA: P.O. Box 609, Fort Erie, Ontario L2A 5X3
Not valid to current subscribers of Love Inspired books.

Want to try two free books from another series?
Call 1-800-873-8635 or visit www.morefreebooks.com

LIREG09

Love Inspired®

Former Chicago cop
Justin Clay thought
the big city was tough.
Until he met his
love-shy neighbor
and her rebellious
teenage nephew. Can
he bring this fractured
family together by
becoming a part of it?

Look for
The Hero
Next Door
by
Irene Hannon

*Available August
wherever books are sold.*

Love Inspired.

The Hero Next Door
Irene Hannon

Lighthouse
L A N E

Lighthouse
L A N E

Steeple
Hill®

LI8754IR

Love Inspired

TITLES AVAILABLE NEXT MONTH

Available July 28, 2009

THE HERO NEXT DOOR by Irene Hannon
Lighthouse Lane

Former Chicago cop Justin Clay thought the big city was tough. Until he meets his love-shy neighbor and her rebellious teenaged nephew. Can he bring this fractured family together by becoming a part of it?

MARRYING MINISTER RIGHT by Annie Jones
After the Storm

Cruelly left at the altar, social worker Heather Waters returns to High Plains, Kansas, her heart tattered like the tornado-ravaged town. Yet as she works with the handsome minister to restore faith, will she discover she's found the man to heal her heart as well?

GIFT OF WONDER by Lenora Worth

Developer Jonah Sheridan vows to rebuild Alice Bryson's hurricane-battered Louisiana bayou community—along with the jilted reporter's broken heart. Winning Alice's trust isn't easy, but Jonah's determined to do whatever it takes to become her honest man.

AN UNEXPECTED MATCH by Dana Corbit
Wedding Bell Blessings

Even their meddling mothers don't think practical single dad Matthew Warren and free-spirited nanny Haley Scott are right for each other. But they surprise everyone—including themselves—by proving that opposites do attract!

HOME AT LAST by Anna Schmidt

Nantucket is the last place Daniel Armstrong wants to settle down. But Jo Cooper, a helper on his mother's cranberry farm, is determined to make Daniel and his teenage daughter see that they've found a home with her.

THE FOREVER FAMILY by Leigh Bale

Single mom Rachel Walker is depending on the kindness of handsome stranger Sam Thorne after she's injured in a Nevada storm. At first Sam is reluctant to help the widow and her child but her strong spirit and gentle faith cause the walls around Sam's heart to come tumbling down.